His destiny awaited in the desert...

"Get down," Tariq commanded in a tone that bore no resistance, and she did so immediately.

The sound of a machine gun tore through the straining rattle of the engine that the driver was pushing to the limit. Sara's brain screamed in disbelief. This couldn't be happening. From the corner of her eye, she saw Tariq return fire, his face hard with concentration, his powerful body focused on the task.

Tariq grabbed her arm and ran with her to the closest cover. He looked at her, his dark eyes swirling with barely restrained rage that softened as he held her gaze, the look turning into something akin to regret.

Then he flattened Sara against a wall and stepped in front of her. Clearly he thought she would be safe here, out of sight.

"I am the sheik. I'm not going to let anything happen to you. I *will* find you when this is over...."

DANA MARTON

SHEIK SEDUCTION

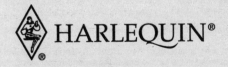

HARLEQUIN®

TORONTO • NEW YORK • LONDON
AMSTERDAM • PARIS • SYDNEY • HAMBURG
STOCKHOLM • ATHENS • TOKYO • MILAN • MADRID
PRAGUE • WARSAW • BUDAPEST • AUCKLAND

With many thanks to Denise Zaza and Allison Lyons.

ISBN-13: 978-0-373-69306-1
ISBN-10:   0-373-69306-0

SHEIK SEDUCTION

ABOUT THE AUTHOR

Author Dana Marton lives near Wilmington, Delaware. She has been an avid reader since childhood and has a master's degree in writing popular fiction. When not writing, she can be found either in her garden or her home library. For more information on the author and her other novels, please visit her Web site at www.danamarton.com.

She would love to hear from her readers via e-mail: DanaMarton@yahoo.com.

Books by Dana Marton

CAST OF CHARACTERS

Sara Reese—She came to the Middle East to do business. But when her convoy is attacked, she finds herself fighting for her life. Can she trust the mysterious sheik who comes to her aid?

Sheik Tariq Abdullah—He wanted Sara from the moment he saw her. But he's afraid she's getting in the way of enemy crossfire. He isn't sure who the bandits are after, but he's prepared to protect her with his life.

Karim Abdullah—Tariq's brother. He lost sight in one eye in an early childhood "accident."

Aziz Abdullah—Karim's twin brother. His leg was permanently injured in the same "accident" that had left Karim blind in one eye.

Omar—Tariq's mentor, the only man he can trust outside his brothers. Or can he?

Husam—A young executive who works for the sheik. He wants Sara for his own. Does he want her enough to kill for it?

Prologue

"Tariq?" the sheika yelled as she ran through the palace, her bare feet slapping on the marble floor. "Have you seen Tariq?" she demanded of the guard at the end of the dark hallway, desperation squeezing her throat.

"Probably playing somewhere." His gaze implied he thought her a hysterical female. He didn't take her seriously.

They never did.

She ran on, knowing she could expect no help from the man—not from him, not from the others. She thought of the two sons she had already lost, and cold fear curled in her stomach. She wept.

"Tariq?" She opened one door after another and tried not to think of Habib, who at the age of four had been found after just such a night, crumpled at the bottom of the stairs.

A sleepwalker, they'd said.

She was his mother. She knew better.

Her giant belly hurt from the mad rush, and she put a hand over it, over the sons who waited to see the world. The sheik was happy.

The sheika had hoped for a girl.

She ran forward, down one corridor, up more stairs. The palace was riddled with passageways: some splendid, some used by servants, others secret and known only to the family. She hated to think of Tariq lost in the maze at night, hunted like a small animal by unseen enemies.

Her child.

Would none of her sons live long enough to pass out of the nursery? She cursed the greed of men, the line of succession and the fact that she was the sheik's favorite wife, garnering more envy than she could defend her children against.

"Allah, let me find him hale tonight." She whispered the same words she had said so many times before.

If Tariq made it past age eight and moved into his father's care, perhaps he would be safe. Nobody would dare touch him that close to the sheik. She would hate to see him go, but was willing to give him up to save him.

She heard footsteps in the darkness and moved silently in the direction of the sound. Small steps.

Tariq. She didn't dare call his name. Heavy boots thumped on the marble behind her.

Her lungs were straining after her desperate race through the palace, and from being squeezed by the babies she carried. The air in the room was thick with the scent of incense that had been burned earlier, making it even harder for her to breathe, to think.

At the last second, she hid behind heavy brocade curtains, and when she saw the five-year-old who was the light of her heart stumble by, she reached out and pulled him in, put a hand over his mouth. He recognized her immediately—by scent or feel, she didn't know. He didn't make a sound. She wrapped her trembling arms around him, stifling the sob of relief that bubbled up her throat.

She had found him in time. *Allah be blessed.*

There was a secret panel behind her. She opened it and slid inside, pressed the wood back into place. Men entered the room, talking.

"Check everywhere. He's small. There, under the divan."

Keeping her arms tight around her son, she willed her heart to still. The men wouldn't know about the secret hiding place. She waited, motionless and silent, clinging to that hope.

But there was a scraping noise on the other side of the panel, and it popped open, a flashlight blinding her. She couldn't see the men who surrounded them. Fear slowed her heart as she slid in front of Tariq. They could only take him if she were dead.

But Tariq pushed forward, putting his small body between her and the men, trying to protect her. The gesture just about broke her heart. She pulled him back.

Tense seconds passed as her eyes adjusted to the light. She wasn't surprised to see her own guard. The captain watched her, and she knew he was thinking about whether two accidental deaths would be one too many for one night.

Four, she thought, sliding one hand off Tariq's shoulder to curl protectively around her stomach.

"There you are," the man said, and moved back, allowing them room to step out. "We received word that Tariq was missing, and came looking for the child."

She moved with effort, her enormous belly slowing her down. Wary of a trap, she didn't dare feel relief, but kept her son close.

"We will return you to your rooms, Sheika. It is careless of you to roam the palace this time of the night."

She nodded, noting how his eyes narrowed with displeasure, the disappointment of an interrupted hunt.

She didn't take an easy breath until she was

inside her quarters, where no man was allowed but her husband, the sheik. She closed the door behind her, locked it, although she knew it mattered little. She wouldn't let Tariq's hand go as she walked around and checked on her daughters, who were sleeping peacefully.

"You sleep with me," she told Tariq.

For once, he didn't argue that he was a big boy and too old for that.

They slipped into bed, and she held him against her, as close as her giant belly allowed. She had to get him out of the palace to save him, she knew.

At the birth of each of her previous sons, the sheik had gifted her with a boon, allowed her a request he'd promised he would not deny. The new babes would come soon. If they were healthy and pleasing to the sheik's eyes…

Tariq had to go far, far away. If even the guards were hunting him now… None of them were safe, perhaps not even the sheik. His successor, a son by the first wife, was impatient for the throne.

But the old man wouldn't see it that way. He had a favorite wife, and also a favorite son. And he was blind to the young sheik's faults.

Little Tariq's body gave a shudder in his sleep. His mother smoothed a hand over his thick, dark hair, hoping he would feel her presence and be calmed even in his dreams.

"Shh." She placed a light kiss on the top of his head. "Whatever I have to do, whatever I have to give, you will be safe."

Chapter One

Thirty years later

She'd been brought here to fail. It was expected of her. Hoped for.

Sara Reeves exited the conference room last, following the men, as was the custom in the region. Jeff had drilled that into her head. Whatever you do, commit no offense. He'd made it clear it was the most important thing he expected of her on this trip, the *only* thing.

"Let us go see the new well," Ahmad Maluk, one of the three directors who represented MMPOIL at today's meeting, said, gesturing toward the bank of elevators. "It'll be a twenty-minute helicopter ride. Miss Reeves is welcome to stay at the hotel and rest if she so wishes."

She wished they could meet the sheik. But they'd already been told that was not going to happen. "I'd love to see the well," she said with respect, talking to no one in particular, not wanting to offend the men by addressing them directly.

"You rest," Jeff said, solicitous as ever. "I can handle it."

He could always handle everything—except the actual work. At schmoozing he was king. Hard to believe there'd been a time when she'd been in love with the man.

"Perhaps we should wait until tomorrow," Husam, the man on Ahmad's left, suggested. He was the youngest of the three Beharrainians, around thirty if that, with a sharp chin and nose, and even sharper eyes that he'd kept on Sara for most of the meeting.

She glanced away, hating the submissive gesture, but knowing that in this culture it was expected of women. One of the slew of oddities that made it difficult for her to stand on even ground for the negotiations.

They should have seen the well and been back by now, but Jeff had had stomach problems that morning and they'd had to delay their meetings. He had used her as an excuse, told everyone she'd been sick. The Arabs put a lot of stock in the strength of a man. If Jeff appeared weak for any reason it would be detrimental to their negotiations. And she could appear a little weaker, so as not to challenge their ideas of women and give offense. The world according to Jeff.

The best thing Sara had ever done for herself was to break their engagement. Unfortunately, untangling their business interests proved more difficult.

Jeff flashed her one of those smiles she had fallen for four years ago, before she'd realized that they, along with most things about him, were fake. "You could go shopping," he said.

With admirable restraint, she kept herself from voicing the response forming on her tongue. "I'd prefer to see the well."

Jeff shrugged with annoyance, but didn't push further. Perhaps he'd given up on trying to manipulate her for the time being.

She zeroed in on the hallway to the left, where she'd seen a sign for a restroom on their way in. Since she knew they would be spending several hours in the desert today, she'd doubled her water intake. "Why don't you go up? I'll be with you in a second." She nodded toward her destination.

Jeff scowled, as if her basic necessities were nothing but feminine whims he was forced to put up with.

She hurried down the hall, trying not to be too paranoid and obsess over what he would say this time to undermine her in her absence. Of course, with this potential customer, the fact that she was a woman was probably enough.

Glancing into the mirror as she exited the

restroom two minutes later, she made sure her insecurities didn't show. B. T. Reeves Studio, a public relations firm specializing in the oil industry, was as much her company as Jeff's—more so, in her opinion. No matter how hard he pushed her, she was not going to relinquish her heritage. She wanted more than anything to regain control of the company and make it a success, a tribute to her father, who had started it.

Husam's dark shape ahead caught her eye, his back half-turned to her. Was he waiting for her? She hadn't liked the way he'd stared at her all through the meeting. She didn't want to be stuck in the close quarters of an elevator with him. He was talking on his cell phone in Arabic, sounding nervous and angry at the same time.

Grateful for the soft carpet, which allowed her to remain undetected, she walked in the other direction. MMPOIL's headquarters was a giant building. There had to be more than one bank of elevators.

She turned the corner and was relieved to see she'd been right. She pushed the call button and held her breath until the bell dinged and the doors opened. They were just starting to close behind her when a man stepped through. For a moment, all she registered was relief that he wasn't Husam.

Oh, my. Definitely not. Wasn't even in the same category.

This guy was close to forty and a good head taller than Husam. He brought a strong sense of presence with him as he stepped inside, so strong his body almost vibrated with intensity. The space in the elevator seemed to shrink, the air thinning all of a sudden.

There was a stark wildness to his masculine features, his tanned face and dark hair. Sara's first impression had been of a hard-set, square jaw and wide shoulders stiff with displeasure, but that seemed to disappear as he watched her. His dark eyes held her gaze.

"Hello." His deeply masculine voice was as spellbinding as the rest of him.

"Hi." She should have looked away politely. She couldn't, even with all her senses suggesting that this guy was several levels above Husam on the danger scale.

Husam hadn't really done anything but stare at her. Maybe he wasn't used to blondes, or women in a negotiating position. She was in a whole new culture. She had to adjust to certain oddities.

She fixed her attention on the closed doors, but couldn't hold it there long before glancing again at the man next to her. He was staring at the sheet of paper in his hand, no longer looking at her, which should have made him seem less intimidating. It didn't.

She acknowledged the fact, but wouldn't let it bother her. She was used to intimidation on a daily basis.

"Do you know if this goes to the helipad?" she asked, unsure whether he would understand her. Anybody could say "*hello*."

"I'll show you when we get up there." His U.S., West Coast accent surprised her. Another American?

"Thanks."

She relaxed marginally, but then her business persona kicked in. "Do you work here or are you visiting?" If MMPOIL had solicited other U.S. companies to bid on the same project she and Jeff were here for, she needed to know.

"I work here," he said, setting her mind at ease.

He folded the paper and slid it into the inner pocket of his suit jacket, then looked at her again. His gaze was sharp and intelligent, intense, but lacking Husam's disquieting intrusion. "Are you here with the Dallas delegation?"

She nodded, wondering how he knew, and what his role was at the company. A subtle, pleasant scent of sandalwood filled the small space and surrounded her. He didn't crowd her as people had tended to do since her arrival—apparently due to their different attitude about personal space—but stood back, detached.

"You work with the sheik?" she asked, registering at last that he hadn't pushed another button. The fiftieth floor was still the only one lit. That meant he was going to the top, as well, which, according to Jeff, was Sheik Abdullah's domain. And also the location of the only elevator that went to the roof. This way, access to the helipad was restricted. For security reasons, she supposed.

The man nodded with a short, deliberate movement of his head, power evident even in such small a gesture as that.

He worked with the sheik. A slide show of romanticized pictures flashed through her mind, straight from the sheik romance novels she'd read. "Is he here today?"

"Yes."

"I suppose he doesn't attend low-level meetings," she said, hiding her chagrin pretty well, she thought.

"He doesn't attend any meetings if he can help it." Her companion had the bearing and self-assurance of a man in charge, but he wasn't among the top tier of executives. Jeff and she had been introduced to them at a reception upon arrival.

She wondered if he might be a close, trusted assistant to the sheik, but his body language and air didn't seem to fit the secretary image. He had a commanding physical presence, his form well-built and powerful. There was a watchful awareness about him that wasn't typical of the average office worker. Nor was his impeccable suit.

And then it clicked. He was probably one of the sheik's bodyguards.

The elevator stopped and he gestured for her to step out first, very atypical of her experience here so far. Maybe he hadn't been in the country long enough for the local attitude to rub off on him. She wondered how long ago he'd been shipped in from the U.S. as a security consultant to the sheik. He had to be good at what he did to be brought all this way.

No doubt about it. She stole another furtive glance, not wanting him to notice her obvious interest. He looked to be the kind of guy who would be good at whatever he did. She couldn't imagine him turning all that intense energy to a purpose and not succeeding.

He gestured at an elevator directly opposite theirs. "That'll take you to the helipad."

He held her gaze for another second, fire and mystery swirling in his dark eyes. *God, this setting was making her ridiculously fanciful.* Then, moving with an inborn elegance, he strode toward the opaque doors that closed off the short hallway from the rest of the floor.

She craned her neck, hoping to catch a glimpse of the sheik's private offices. It would be neat to see a real-life sheik. She'd been disappointed when she'd realized their itinerary didn't include meeting the man.

"What is he like, the sheik?" she couldn't help calling after him. She pictured Sheik Abdullah in flowing white robes edged with gold, a kaffiyeh on his head, looking fiercely royal, surrounded by the splendor of his station. She was a little sketchy on the splendor part. Sometimes it showed up in her imagination as a gilded room in some palace, other times as a tent with priceless Persian rugs, set up at a breathtaking oasis in the middle of the desert.

He turned toward her and said, "Not someone you'd want to meet."

Was that amusement glinting in his eyes?

"He's a morose bastard." He placed a tanned hand on the door. "Enjoy your time in Beharrain, Miss Reeves," he said before he slipped through.

She blinked, then shook her head slightly and walked to the elevator, refusing to feel guilty for having made the men wait. She squared her shoulders as she stepped in, getting ready for the subtle manipulations she would have to deal with on the way to the well. Jeff was going to do everything he could to pressure her into remaining in the background at tomorrow's presentation. She wasn't going to let him. Nor would she ever allow him to get his hands on her share of the company.

Would he eventually give up?

But as the elevator door opened to the roof, and oppressive heat surrounded her, a second question popped into her mind, for a moment overriding the first. How did the sheik's bodyguard know her name?

MAYBE SHE *SHOULD* HAVE gone back to the hotel. The temperature had to be well over a hundred degrees outside. The Hummer they'd taken was air-conditioned, but heat radiated through the window next to her.

They should have been at the well long ago, but the corporate helicopter had some problems, and the decision had been made to go by car. No more than a three-hour drive, they'd been assured. Sara's teeth were still on edge from her fifteen-minute conversation with Jeff, who'd used this as an excuse to mount a new offensive, doing what he could to convince her to stay behind.

She sat next to him now, trying not to look at Husam. He had insisted on keeping them company on the road, while a second Hummer transported two other men from MMPOIL who were supposed to take the same chopper, plus two armed guards. The fact that bodyguards were necessary didn't exactly put her at ease.

One sat in her vehicle, as well, next to Husam. The man from the elevator. He'd shown up at the last second—Tariq somebody. The driver had started the engine just as he got in, so she didn't catch his full name.

"Water?" he was asking in that deeply masculine voice, pulling a bottle of Evian from the cooler and pointing toward the glasses.

"Yes, please," she said.

Jeff shook his head. Husam declined with a respectful bow and an odd look on his face. Maybe he thought the direct contact between them was impolite.

Tariq poured, then handed her the glass, which she took very carefully to make sure they didn't touch—according to her guide book that was a big no-no around here.

The man poured for himself, as well. He sat opposite her, the seats facing each other, and seemed to command Husam's deference. At least the latter left plenty of room between them. Tariq was working directly with Sheik Abdullah, after all, and probably had the sheik's ear. Other than respectfully greeting the newcomer when he arrived, Husam had not attempted to talk to him, though his appearance had clearly surprised him.

He even refrained from staring at Sara for the most part, which was fine by her. She hadn't been overjoyed when she'd realized that they would be riding together.

"I love this car," Jeff said in an overly cheerful

tone. "Custom? Always said that the H2 and H3 can't be compared to the H1 Alpha wagon."

Husam perked up and the two embarked on a discussion about Hummers that she only intermittently understood. Which left her plenty of time to ponder her companions.

It seemed laughable now that a few hours ago she'd felt threatened by Husam. Next to Tariq, he seemed insignificant. Even Jeff, who was handsome in a softer, city-boy sort of way—he'd certainly gotten around among the women at the company office—couldn't hold a candle to Tariq, whose raw masculinity seemed to jump across the short gap that separated his knees from hers.

She wished he would join the conversation so she could find out more about him and the man he worked for, but he seemed lost in the contents of the folder he'd brought along. Probably for the best. When he did look at her, his intensity made her feel painfully self-conscious, anyway.

"Any Bedouins around here?" Jeff asked, pronouncing the word "bad ones," a private joke he'd made several times since they'd arrived, thinking nobody noticed.

But Sara saw the muscles tighten in Tariq's jaw. If he took offense, however, he gave no other sign of it, didn't even look up.

"Farther in the desert to the south," Husam said.

She glanced out the window.

There was no road, only a faint track that wasn't bad when they were going over sand. But when they hit rocky areas, she was afraid her kidneys would be shaken to bits by the time they reached their destination. She wanted to ask how much farther they had to go, but would have bitten off her tongue before doing so. If the men weren't bothered by the ride, then she was prepared to pretend that she wasn't, either.

She looked out over the dunes, daydreaming about Bedouin raids of the past, about horses flying over the sand, the treasures of the East packed on camelback, the shouts, the braying, the clashing of swords. Then she bit back a smile. Clearly, she'd read too many historical romances.

She wondered if Abdullah was anything like the sheiks of old, and the image of a breathtaking warrior atop a black Arabian stallion floated into her mind. But that picture was quickly replaced by the very real appearance of a beat-up military truck, the first sign of life they'd seen since they had entered the desert.

"Are we here?" she asked, full of hope.

Both Tariq and Husam were staring out the window, Husam's face inscrutable, while Tariq's grew dark as he reached behind his seat and came up with a handgun.

"What's going on?" Her voice went squeaky, her heart thumping at the sight of the weapon.

"Get down," Tariq commanded in a tone that bore no argument, and she did so immediately, putting her head between her knees.

"Oh, my God, oh, my God," Jeff was saying, and did the same. "What's happening? Are those bandits?"

Bandits? The air left Sara's lungs. Nobody had said anything about bandits. Beharrain was supposed to be safe and a friend of the U.S., thanks to its American-born queen. That was one of the reasons Sara's company had decided to do business here instead of some other country in the region.

Couldn't be bandits. She'd seen those beat-up old army trucks all over the city. People bought them after they'd been decommissioned by the military, and used them for everything from furniture moving to selling Middle Eastern fast food on the streets.

The sound of a round from a machine gun—the truck was definitely not selling melon sherbet— sounded over the growling rattle of the Hummer's engine, which the driver was pushing to the limit now. *Bandits!* her brain screamed in disbelief, as she shrunk instinctively, trying to make herself as small a target as possible.

From the corner of her eye she saw Tariq roll down the window and return fire. Spent shells pinged to the floor at her feet. *Oh, God, oh, God, help us.* An acrid smell lingered in the air, which after a moment she realized was the smell of gun-powder from the weapon's discharge.

Blood rushed in her ears, and her body vibrated with her growing panic. This couldn't be happening. Had to be a dream.

On her first night in the country, she'd had a torrid dream of being abducted by a mysterious sheik, a story line straight out of a book. Now she was dreaming about a bandit attack because she'd been watching the regional news, which had reported the kidnapping of a group of journalists in Yemen, across the border. The terror around her couldn't be real. The front desk would be ringing with her wake-up call any minute now.

Instead, their car slowed, sending her panic into higher gear. She glanced up and caught a glimpse of the driver draped over the steering wheel, half of his face missing. She squeezed her eyes shut, holding her breath.

"I think I'm going to be sick," she said, but nobody was paying attention to her.

Tariq exchanged some words with Husam in Arabic as the vehicle rolled to a halt in the sand. Maybe he was Beharrainian, after all. Or Beharrainian-American. She tried to focus on that instead of on the bile rising in her throat as she lurched to the floor, whimpering when bullets sprayed the side of their Hummer.

Jeff tumbled from the vehicle on the other side. "We have to run for it."

She followed him out, then flattened herself on the sand, using the tires for cover.

The attacking truck was coming closer, Tariq still firing from his seat, his face a mask of concentration as he focused on the task. The scene would have easily fit into an action movie—*dashing hero saving the day.* Except that even motion picture heroes couldn't win against an opposing force this overwhelming. A second truck had appeared behind the first.

Fear pushed her to flee from what she knew to be certain death. But where? Husam was outside now, keeping low to the ground and running. The driver of the first Hummer had realized that the second one had been disabled, and turned around, coming back for them.

"Let's go for it." Jeff grabbed her by the arm and pulled her up.

For a moment she hesitated, too scared to leave their cover. But maybe he was right. Husam had nearly reached the other vehicle already. Maybe they, too, could make it to relative safety. The Hummer was lighter and faster than the trucks. They might be able to outrun the attackers.

She pushed herself to her feet and sprinted forward, focusing on their goal. If she looked around, if she considered for even a moment the massacre surrounding her, she would have frozen, providing an easy target for the next bullet.

"Don't stop. Don't stop. Keep low," Tariq yelled from behind them, covering them as best he could.

They were twenty feet away when Jeff stumbled and dragged her down with him. The sand scorched her bare palms as she put them out for support.

"Come on. Get up." She pulled, keeping an eye on the beat-up military truck, which was dangerously close. When Jeff didn't move, she glanced at him. His eyes were gazing into the distance, a frozen look on his face. He was dead, his fingers still locked around her arm. "Jeff?"

Dead. Gone. She stared at him, immobilized by mind-numbing horror, barely registering the sight of two men jumping off the back of the still-moving truck and running for her.

They wore camouflage uniforms, their heads completely covered with white headdresses. By the time she was fully cognizant of the danger and could act again it was too late. One of them grabbed her, rough fingers digging into her flesh, yanking her away from Jeff's prone body on the sand. "No! Let me go!"

The other reached for her, too, but then crumpled to the ground with a surprised expression on his face. She spun around and saw Tariq running toward them. Her captor welcomed him with bullets.

Everything was happening too fast. She couldn't think, didn't know what to do, which way to run.

Blood spread on Tariq's arm. He slowed, his expression even fiercer, more determined than before. He didn't look like the type of man who would give up while his heart beat in his chest. And neither could she.

"Get away from me!" She whipped back to face her captor, kicking and screaming, though she knew it was useless. Tariq wasn't going to reach her. She was only delaying the inevitable.

Sara had always wanted to see the desert. Now she had done so. It wasn't nearly as romantic as she had thought. The place was scary and dangerous, and dashing heroes didn't ride about saving damsels in distress.

"No!" She fought with her nails and teeth, her feet and elbows, even attempted to butt the man with her head. But her efforts were neutralized as easily as if she were a child. Bodies littered the sand now. She would be next, she thought, nearly hysterical with fear and breathless from her efforts.

She should be dead already, she realized then, in a moment of clarity. The bandits could have shot her at any time. They hadn't. They wanted to take her. The recognition brought a fresh wave of panic. "What do you want from me?"

As she twisted away from her attacker, she expected to see Tariq sprawled on the sand next to the others. But miraculously, he was still coming. The sight of him, bloodied but unde-terred, gave her new strength to claw at the menacing, gap-toothed bandit who held her in a viselike grip.

"You're not gonna take me!" she grunted. "Let me go!"

Then Tariq was there, finally, and her captor fell dead at her feet the next second. Tariq grabbed her arm and ran with her toward the other Hummer, the closest cover. Bullets flew all around them, from men who fought on the sand and those who'd stayed on the trucks.

She ducked behind the car when they reached it, hoping there'd be someone there to join, to gain strength from numbers. But nobody was alive save for her and Tariq, and the vehicle had been shot to oblivion.

"Why are they doing this?"

Tariq didn't answer. He was too busy returning fire.

His arm was covered in blood. He'd lost too much. How long would he be able to keep up the fight? Sara planned to take the gun from him and continue shooting if he wavered, but the handgun clicked with his next shot. Empty.

He glanced at her, his dark eyes swirling with barely restrained rage that softened as he held her gaze, the look turning into something akin to regret.

This was it, she thought. As good as he was, he could do no more without firepower. They had seconds at most before the bandits reached them. And then... She couldn't bear thinking about what would happen next. Her mind was filled with the gruesome images of the men who had been mercilessly massacred already. Jeff...

Sand flew up around them. The bandits had plenty of ammunition and were not afraid to use it.

"Take off your jewelry." Tariq cast his useless weapon aside, then rolled up his sleeves to pull off an expensive watch. He buried it in the sand, along with his cell phone, which had the *No Signal* message on its display. "Quick," he said when she hesitated, wondering about his request.

She slipped off her two rings, although, facing certain death, those few grams of gold were the last things she was worried about.

He brushed sand over them, as well.

The bandits were shouting and moving closer, emboldened by the lack of return fire.

Fear squeezed her lungs, so tight she could hardly breathe. She dipped her head when a bullet came too close, and could all of a sudden see the oncoming attack through the gap above the tire. For a moment she was struck speechless, but then she asked, with all the desperation she felt. "What do they want from us?"

She didn't get to find out. Something hard connected with the back of her head and her world went dark.

Chapter Two

"Are the charges set?" He looked at the pumps dispassionately. For a man to reach his goals, sacrifices had to be made. A goal as large as his required an equally large sacrifice.

"Everything is ready, Shah. We are just waiting for the young sheik to leave and the workers to go on break. He wasn't expected here today."

How fortunate that he had come, anyway. "Detonate."

"Now?" The idiot was staring at him, wide-eyed with sudden fear and lack of understanding.

He simply glared at the gaunt young man. He was *not* going to have his orders questioned.

"Yes, Shah," the man said after a long pause, his face several shades whiter than a few moments ago. He scurried off to the utility trailer where he'd worked for the past three months and disappeared inside.

The explosion that shook the desert with elemental force was followed by another, then another, the charges going off in neat order, obliterating the target and everyone around it.

He watched the clouds of sand with satisfaction, then the flames that shot to the sky. His man appeared as the dust settled, running for him, for the car. The shah lifted his pistol and aimed carefully. His ears were still ringing from the explosion, so he barely heard the shot. But he allowed himself, at last, a satisfied smile. It wouldn't be long now before he would reclaim for his son what was rightfully his and fulfill their family's destiny.

SARA WOKE WITH A HEADACHE, her mouth so parched her tongue was stuck to the roof of her mouth. Sand, as fine as dust, ground between her teeth.

She opened her eyes, grateful for the shade of the busted Hummer she was leaning against. She lifted a hand to the back of her head and winced as her fingertips came in contact with a nasty bump.

Motionless bodies lay scattered on the sand. Fear and confusion washed over her as memories of the attack came back in a rush.

"Oh, God." The words tore from her throat, followed by a horrified groan.

Faint clanging drew her attention, and she swung toward the sound, but it stopped almost as soon as it began. She pushed herself to standing and sneaked a peek over the car's roof. The military trucks were nowhere to be seen. A man was working on the other Hummer, his upper body half-under the hood.

She recognized his powerful physique and the determination in his focused movements. *Tariq.*

She wasn't alone. Thank God, she wasn't alone.

"Excuse me," she called out, her voice so raw she didn't think he would hear her.

But he turned and glanced at her. "You're awake. Good." He scrutinized her with narrowed eyes.

She moved forward. Maybe all hope wasn't lost yet. She stumbled to the closest man and sank onto her knees in front of him, turned his head, blanched at the fixed, empty stare, the dark lashes clumped with blood. The driver of the other Hummer. She recognized him before her gaze fell to his ring finger, which had been hacked off.

Tariq's voice was tight as he spoke. "They're all dead. I already checked."

She drew her hands back. The sun was cooking her, the sand burning everywhere she touched it. A wave of dizziness assailed her. She was going to be sick, or faint or have a nervous breakdown. Surely all of those responses would have been appropriate under the circumstances.

"Have you called for help?" she asked weakly.

Maybe he had walked around and found a spot where his phone worked.

"There's no signal this far out. And they took the satellite phones from the cars. Took everything that could be sold at the nearest market. Get out of the sun."

She stumbled back to the car to see if she could find some water, glanced through the window and gagged at the sight. One of the armed guards sprawled across the backseat, bathed in blood. Lots of it. She pushed away and lurched toward Tariq, fixing her eyes on the sand at her feet, not wanting to see any more dead.

He glanced at her when she stopped next to him. "You should drink."

She couldn't form the words to respond. Hardship on a business trip before had meant that the projector didn't work. What had happened here was beyond all comprehension. She couldn't begin to process and make sense of it.

She ran a hand over her body, scarcely able to believe that she had survived whole. Her brown skirt was speckled with dark stains, her top had been torn. She had bought the suit specifically for this trip because the skirt was longer than usual, the outfit suitably modest. She reached to her blouse, and found it stiff with dried blood. Not her blood; nothing hurt when she moved.

A faint sound in the distance startled her, and she launched herself against Tariq's solid chest, thinking another attack imminent. Then she realized it was only the wind. She stepped back, embarrassed, away from the steadying hand he held out.

"Do you think they'll return?" Her voice was shaky from nerves.

The look he gave her was an understanding one. "I don't see why they would, but we better get out of here, anyway." He walked around and pulled out a bottle of Evian from the back. He even twisted off the cap for her, before coming back and handing it over. "We're lucky this rolled under the driver's seat."

"Thank you." She drank sparingly, then tried to give the bottle back, but he wouldn't take it.

Instead, he reached out and cradled her cheek in his hand, lifted her chin and rubbed something from her jaw with his thumb. Dry blood, most likely. The moment dragged out, and she stood still, surprised by the gesture, even a little breathless.

"You'll be fine. Go sit behind the car, in the shade," he said gruffly when he finally spoke.

His simple touch of comfort helped to ease her shock and fear. After a moment he let his hand drop, but she was reluctant to move away. She felt better near him, as if his strength somehow extended beyond his body.

He said nothing, but went back to work on the engine, wiggling a wire with one long finger until he got it into the position he'd been apparently aiming for. "This should work." He went around, reached through the driver's side window and turned the key. The motor came to life.

The sweetest sound she had ever heard. Her eyes nearly teared up with relief.

He shut it off almost immediately.

"You should sit and rest." He pointed to the small patch of shade the car provided.

She looked at him, then to the car, noticing that he had already cleared out the back—no bodies there. Nor anything else. Their briefcases were missing. Hers had held her laptop, cell phone, all her money, her passport and her plane tickets. She sank to the sand. It was marginally cooler in the shade.

Tariq walked back to the front and slammed the hood, which had to be hot enough to fry eggs *and* sausage.

"Why did they do this to us?" she asked.

He gave her question some thought, although she was sure he must have considered it himself while he'd worked on the motor. "Could be we were at the wrong place at the wrong time."

"Who were they?" She tried to rub dried blood off her hands.

He shrugged, the movement filled with tension.

"Gun trade has been a profitable business in this part of the desert for the last couple of decades. Sex trade's fading, but as long as there's still some money in it, it won't be completely abandoned. Drugs are always a possibility."

Outrage unfurled inside Sara and nudged her out of her shell-shocked state. If they knew this, how could MMPOIL have brought them here? "So this happens all the time?"

"Not in the last four years, since the country stabilized," he said darkly.

All she could think of was that they should have waited for the chopper to be fixed. She tried to make sense of the events of the past hour as Tariq took off two shot-up tires and replaced one with the spare, the other with an unharmed one from the other Hummer, refusing her offer of help. Then he got a short-handled shovel from the back and began digging in the sand a few yards from the vehicle.

She watched the shimmering horizon, petrified that the attackers would return. Only when the sound of digging stopped did she look back at Tariq. He seemed to be swaying. The heat of the sun was powerful.

"Are you okay?" She got up and walked to him, holding out the half-empty water bottle.

Instead of responding, he went back to digging again.

"I can help," she said.

"Go back to the car."

The arm of his dark blue shirt was soaking wet, she realized for the first time. Blood trickled down the back of his hand onto the shovel. And she remembered now that he'd been shot when he'd come to save her. How could she have forgotten that? She could barely think with all this death and destruction around them.

"You're bleeding." She handed him the water, trying to examine his arm.

"It's fine," he said through gritted teeth, but stopped for a second to take a few measured gulps.

"I'll dig. You could bring over the bodies." Now that the grave was taking shape, she'd finally figured out what he was trying to do.

She reached for the shovel, and at first he pulled away. But then he let her have it with a faint nod of appreciation, and started across the sand.

She could have been digging in talcum powder, she soon discovered. The sand flowed where it pleased, slowing her progress. She tried not to look at the dead as Tariq dragged them over one by one, but saw enough to register that they were all men who'd come with them. Her breath left her, her chest tightening painfully when she saw Jeff.

Jeff was dead. Jaw clenched tight, Sara kept digging.

It had been years since they'd been lovers, and God knew, they hadn't been the best of friends lately. But they had history. She had been ready to have him out of her life for good, but not this way. She'd been hoping to scrape together enough money to buy him out. She felt the first tear roll down her face, quickly followed by an army of others that evaporated in the heat before they could reach her chin.

Tariq was by her side, taking the shovel from her. "Go back to the shade."

Seven bodies lay in a neat row. She knelt next to Jeff and untucked her shirt to wipe his face with the clean part, straightened his tie and jacket, smoothed down his blondish hair.

She barely recognized her own voice, it sounded so hollow when she spoke. "Where are the rest?" She'd seen more men than this die in the fierce battle.

"The smugglers took their own. Cleaning up evidence." He tossed the shovel aside and dragged the bodies into the shallow, wide grave, one after the other.

She helped as best she could, pushing sand over the fallen with her bare hands while Tariq used the shovel. At the end, he said a few words in Arabic, and she added a simple prayer, said a teary goodbye to Jeff. When she was done, she followed Tariq back to the car.

He picked up the driver's kaffiyeh, then went to the other Hummer and brought a suit coat from there, laying them on the grave. "It's an old Bedu custom, to pass on the clothes of the dead to some poor wanderer."

"They were Bedouin?" She couldn't consolidate the sharp business suits with her idea of desert nomads.

"We are all Bedu," he said as they got into the car.

She tried to picture him in a goat-hair tent. It didn't work. That West Coast accent threw her off.

"We can tell the families where they are," she said as he put the vehicle into motion, feeling guilty for being alive. "The bodies can be found again, right? The other Hummer will be here."

He drove in silence for a few moments before he responded. "My people are at rest. We believe that we come from the desert, so we go back to the desert when we die. No marked graves. The sand is sufficient."

It did seem fitting. The vast desert in itself was a breathtaking monument. She was sure, however, that Jeff's parents would want his body to be returned to the States. Guilt pushed deeper into her core. It didn't seem fair that all these people had died and she was alive. Not that she didn't feel grateful. She did. Then felt guilty about the quiet appreciation that she was still here to draw hot air into her lungs.

"How about the GPS?" Both Hummers were well equipped. "Don't those things have panic buttons or locators or whatever?"

"The other one was shot to bits. This one I had hope for…." He gestured at the display, at the small hole in the middle, then shook his head, his masculine lips pressed in a flat line.

From his expression she figured the damage was bad enough to render the unit unusable.

"Where are we going?" she asked after a while. "What's closer, Tihrin or the well we were heading for?"

"Wouldn't make it to either. A bullet nicked the oil pan. We have a slow leak."

She looked at the profusion of holes in the door next to her and the dashboard before her. Everyone had been trying to take cover behind the vehicles, which had taken the brunt of the attack. That Tariq had been able to salvage one of them was a miracle.

"Without oil to lubricate the engine, it'll overheat and stop. If we're lucky, we'll make it as far as the oasis," he said. "We need more water. And we should get out of the open as fast as possible."

She pictured palm trees nodding in the wind, green grass and a glistening blue pool where some underground stream surfaced in the sand. She would have given anything to be able to wash off the blood.

"Can we get in touch with the sheik somehow? He could send people to get us out of here." She pictured robed men racing over the sand on beautiful horses, their swords drawn, the sheik at the very front. They would be brave and fierce, whisking her to safety.

She blinked that image away. Okay, so reality would most likely be a group of the sheik's armed guards, sent in the chopper—when someone fixed it. Either way, she would be deliriously happy to see anyone who came to the rescue.

The look on Tariq's face redefined grim. "In case this wasn't a random attack, we need to figure out whom we can trust, before we do anything. But yes, there is a satellite phone at the oasis."

She let herself relax a little. "I'm sure you can trust the sheik and the people at your company. And the authorities."

She didn't want to sit around in a desert full of murderers any longer than was absolutely neces-sary. The people they'd buried were an effective reminder just how dangerous the place was.

"We buried only seven," she realized belatedly. "There were ten of us. Who's missing?" She'd tried as much as she could not to look at the bodies as they'd buried the men.

"They took Husam. Perhaps he was injured at the end and could no longer fight. I didn't see him."

"And they tried to take me. Why?"

"Husam's father is a wealthy man. They might have recognized the son. Could be they wanted you for themselves, or to sell at Yanadar or to ransom you to your foreign family." Tariq's face was getting darker and darker as he spoke.

Her chest tightened at the prospects he was enumerating. *Yanadar?* Did that have something to do with the sex trade he'd mentioned? She rubbed her arm where she'd been grabbed, and found her skin still tender. "But then why didn't they take me? At the end?" She fingered the bump on the back of her head. She certainly couldn't have defended herself.

"They thought you were dead." He paused a beat. "Sorry about that."

For a moment she didn't understand. Then the hard object that had hit her made sense all of a sudden. He'd been the only person near enough to hurt her. He'd still had his gun back then. "You hit me?"

"I couldn't be sure if you could pull off playing dead. I had no bullets left. They were closing in."

He'd knocked her out, then draped his bleeding body over her and pretended the bandits had shot both of them. There'd certainly been enough blood to be convincing.

"I still don't see what they would want with me. If they were going for ransom, why not grab Jeff, too? The sex slave thing…" She shook her head. "Seems too far-fetched, frankly."

"Don't count on it." He dug into his pocket, then held her rings out on his open palm. He could afford to take his attention off the road now. They were going over flat terrain, and it wasn't as if he would cross the center line and veer into oncoming traffic.

"Thanks…for saving these," she said, although her jewelry was pretty low on her list of priorities at the moment. She noticed suddenly that his watch was already on his wrist. He must be attached to it, she decided.

"If they saw anything valuable on either of us, they would have taken it. And if they had to grab us and move us around, they might have realized we weren't dead. Or they would have…" He fell silent and looked back at the so-called road.

Would have what? She was about to ask when she thought of the driver with his finger missing. She nodded, grateful that Tariq had had the presence of mind to think of everything.

"Husam was at your meeting this morning?" he asked. "The more I think about it, the less I believe this could have been a random attack. They might have known he was coming, and lain in wait for him."

"What about the two men in the other car?"

He thought for a second. "Minor managers.

And nobody tried to take them. They were shot in cold blood."

"An assassination? Maybe they were the true target."

"But then why take Husam? I think that's the real clue," Tariq said.

She tended to agree with him. "When the others went up to the helipad, he stayed behind to make a call. He sounded…I don't know. I didn't understand anything he was saying. But he sounded angry and stressed. Maybe he told whoever he was talking to that he was headed for the desert. Maybe he was betrayed?" She didn't much care for Husam, but she hated to think of anyone in the hands of ruthless bandits. God knew what they would do to him.

"Possible," Tariq said, tight-lipped. "Did he know at that time that you'd be taking the cars instead of the chopper? You were still heading for the roof when we met."

"I was told as soon as I got up there that the helicopter needed repairs. Someone could have called him already. Maybe that's why he never went up."

"Was there anything strange about your leaving? Do you remember him talking to anyone else in the hallway? Have you noticed anyone watching him?"

"No, but at the meeting…" She hesitated, not wanting to sound like a complete idiot.

"At the meeting?" Tariq's gaze was sharp as he studied her face.

"He was looking at me. A lot."

His expression softened, a corner of his mouth turning up. "For that, you must forgive us."

Meaning what? That he thought Husam liked the way she looked, and maybe he shared that feeling? Husam's interest left her cold, but the possibility that Tariq would be attracted to her sent heat skittering through her. There had to be another explanation to his words. She wasn't about to ask.

She remembered another detail. "We were supposed to visit the well this morning. When we were delayed, Husam recommended that we not go until tomorrow. Jeff wouldn't hear of it. Maybe Husam had a premonition."

Tariq tapped his long fingers on the steering wheel as he considered that. "Why was Husam with you, but none of the others you met with?"

"The site supervisor was expecting us. We were supposed to take the chopper without escort. Husam decided only midmeeting that he would come along."

They drove in silence for a while, until Tariq leaned forward and narrowed his eyes, gesturing toward the horizon. "The oasis. We are almost there."

She stared ahead through the steam that rose from under the hood. Then stared harder still as the scene unfolded before them. Instead of the tourist picture her mind had conjured, straight ahead was an abandoned construction site in the middle of nowhere, a ghost town of steel and cement.

Tariq slowed and looked toward the west for a long moment, making her nervous. Did he see something? She searched the distance, looking for any dark spots that might be approaching trucks.

"What? What do you see?" Dread and fear were choking her. *Don't let it be bandits! Anything but that.*

But when he spoke, the news he shared with her was even more frightening, his voice as grim as his expression.

"We better hurry. There's a sandstorm coming," he said as he stepped on the gas.

Chapter Three

He wasn't the sort of man who dealt well with failure. Seeing the abandoned construction site that had been his pet project set Tariq's teeth on edge. Yet it was nothing but a minor annoyance compared to the rage that he felt over the attack, over his men being killed, over Sara Reeves being put in danger. He was mad at himself, too, for not anticipating it, for being unable to do more.

The Hummer was barely rolling. At this stage, they would have moved faster on foot, but he didn't want to abandon the vehicle in plain sight.

"This is the oasis?" Sara stared at him with incredulity in her expressive blue eyes that said she found the place hideous.

She, on the other hand, was beautiful, even covered with sand and blood. And what kind of man was he to notice things like that after what had just happened to his men?

"It will be," he stated. He didn't need one more person to question or make fun of his enterprise, whether she had the most beguiling eyes he'd ever seen or not. "Who was Jeff Myers to you?"

More than a business partner; on that Tariq would stake his life. He'd seen the way the man had looked at Sara when he thought nobody was watching.

She glanced away. "An old friend."

He waited.

"We were supposed to get married. B. T. Reeves was my father's company. Jeff brought needed capital and got half the firm for it. I inherited the other half after cancer took Dad." She pressed her lips together as if she'd said too much. "Everything was supposed to work out perfectly with the two of us getting married." She seemed compelled to explain, anyway.

"Except the wedding never happened." Tariq wanted to know why, realized this wasn't the time to ask.

"Where is the water?" She seemed eager to move off the subject.

There'd been plenty of tension between her and her partner; Tariq had read that clearly in the car before the attack. Judging from the man's quiet resentment and sullen attempts to dominate her, she must have been the one who'd broken off the relationship. Jeff Meyers had wanted to regain control, probably to get her back. Tariq couldn't blame him.

He thought of the tender way she had buried the man she no longer loved, no longer even liked, if their earlier interaction was any indication. But she had worried that his body should be found for his family. She was loyal to the end.

And right now, she was gazing at Tariq expectantly.

Yes, the water. "Under the sand."

He pulled the Hummer inside one of the buildings, which had walls standing but no doors or windows yet. They hadn't gotten that far with the project.

She jumped out. "There aren't any palm trees."

Her innocent remark pricked him more sharply than it should have.

He wasn't daft; nobody needed to explain to him what an oasis should look like. Tariq tempered his irritation. He was getting too sensitive about this venture and all the questions that still swirled around it in the media—damaging publicity financed by his enemies.

"Can't put in landscaping until all the heavy machinery is out of here." He saw the place as it would be when the work was completed, this room a banquet hall fit for the most discriminating guests. He shook off the sense of frustration as he strode out the back of the building.

"It's not what I expected." She trailed after him.

He'd spent his life escaping other people's expectations. He wasn't about to start worrying about hers, regardless of whatever unreasonable attraction he felt for her. "The oasis will be a resort with a capital *O*."

"Ah," she said, but appeared uncertain still, her face softening, giving him a glimpse of what she was like with her defenses down. Of course, every expression was appealing on Sara Reeves.

"There was a real oasis here, but the well dried up about fifty years ago." He searched for the best place to weather the storm, noticing as he did so that the satellite dish was missing. Probably knocked down by the unusually savage storm they'd had a week ago. "When we were looking for a site for a new project and had some surveys done, we found plenty of water. The water table is now deep below the bottom of the well our ancestors dug in the sand." The desert had gotten drier and drier over the last century.

"So you're from around here?" She gave him a searching look. "You talk like an American."

"I lived in the States for a while." Sometimes he thought it'd been too long, sometimes too short. He watched as her gaze flitted over his buildings. She didn't seem impressed. It annoyed him more than it should.

"MMPOIL is branching out?" she asked.

"The oil won't last forever."

Now was the time to set up other businesses, to start to develop other industries. His people's future depended on these initiatives, and he took them seriously, even though he'd received plenty of ridicule as a result. His generation had grown up oil rich. They'd seen nothing else, could imagine nothing else. They couldn't fathom that the revenue and the lifestyle it brought would ever end. And if any such unpleasant thought did cross their minds, they took care of it with a shrug and an *insha'Allah*—it'll be according to Allah's will.

"This place is huge." She looked back at him finally. She had eyes the shade of the desert sky right after a rare rain took all the sand particles out of the air. A captivating blue that brightened further the few times she let her guard down, never longer than seconds at a time.

The top of her head was even with his nose. She was slim but strong, inside and out. She might bend, but she wouldn't break. She had nearly maimed the bandit who'd grabbed her.

Tariq forced his gaze away from her lips, which might look soft if she ever relaxed. "Twenty acres. Someday it'll be a five-star resort that will draw visitors from all over the world."

He also had a convention center complex in

mind for another location, closer to Tihrin, and a long list of other projects he fought with his enemies to bring to fruition. All things that were suddenly low on his list of priorities.

He headed toward the cluster of luxury villas, the most completed buildings. No doors or windows here, either, but the floors were tiled and the roofs finished, the sunken pools in the bathrooms set up with plumbing, if not yet hooked up to water.

"Wow, this is amazing," Sara said, with a fair dose of surprise in her voice as she took in the brilliant colors of the mosaic tiles depicting scenes from nature, similar to those at the ancient ruins to the west of them.

"We'll get water and look for the satellite dish." The latter had to be near the tall building it'd rested on, probably buried in sand. They had used it during construction to amplify cell phone signals, since the nearest tower was so far away. Tariq needed to talk to his brothers, and let Omar, Husam's father, know about his son's abduction, although the kidnappers might have contacted him by now.

Tariq sympathized with the anguish the man must be in, and to a degree, he blamed himself. He should have noticed when the bandits took Husam, and done something to prevent it. He owed as much to Omar, an old family friend who had been there for Tariq's father until the end. But Tariq had been so focused on Sara, and sure that Husam could hold his own…. No time to dwell on all that now. Before he could be of any help to Husam, he first had to save Sara and himself.

Water. Satellite dish. Car.

If for some reason he couldn't get a connection, he would fix the Hummer with whatever scraps he could scrounge, and take Sara to the nearest town as soon as the storm blew over.

"You work with the sheik, you must have his direct line," she was saying. "Even if you think someone from your company might be involved, we could tell him to send only his most trusted men."

She'd be surprised to know just how few trusted men the sheik had. "Stay here," Tariq murmured.

The building provided shade, the windows strategically placed so that even without air-conditioning the cross breeze would bring relief to the occupants. He moved through the villa, squinting against the sun when he stepped outside and headed for the trailers the workers had used before they left. Padlocked. He strode back to the Hummer for the tire iron and used it to bust the lock on one door.

The four cots inside made for cramped quarters, and the air was stale, still carrying the smell of sweat that clung to the bedding. He dug through a tin chest at the foot of one bed and took the single clean blanket. His next stop was the canteen. There, he got a twenty-liter pot, used the tire iron to break the Plexiglas in the vending machine, and filled the container nearly to the brim with small packages of snacks, before returning to the villa.

"Hungry?"

She was sitting on the floor with her back against the wall, eyeing the food he carried.

He tossed the blanket onto the floor and spread it out with her help, then poured his loot in the middle. "I'll go get water." And he'd keep an eye out for that satellite dish. On the off chance he had been the main target of the attack, he wanted to warn his brothers. If someone was after control of MMPOIL, they would be next.

"What can I do to help?" She stood gracefully, although she had to be exhausted both physically and emotionally. She walked to the door with him.

"See if there's anything left in the car we might need while we're here." He hurried toward the main water pipe, keeping her in his line of sight as she made her way back to the Hummer.

She disappeared inside the building only briefly, soon coming back into view with what looked like an armload of garbage.

When the pot was filled, Tariq started to return,

but something caught his eye near an outlying building.

"I'll go look around," he called out, waiting until she reached the villa before he did so. His gaze settled on the shapeless business suit she wore— probably in deference to the customs of his country. Idly, he wondered how she dressed at home, in her own element. His mind readily skipped to form- fitting, skin-revealing outfits he'd seen plenty of during his time in California.

He thought of those years with nostalgia. Noth- ing would ever be that simple for him again. He had grown an impenetrable shell in the four years since he'd been back in Beharrain, an armor needed to protect him from his enemies, from the pain of betrayals. Only lately had he been realizing that while it served its purpose of staving off attacks, his shield was also beginning to imprison him.

He set the water down and strode toward the distant lines in the sand. Sara Reeves had asked him to send for his most trusted men. Truth was, he did not, could not, trust anyone except Omar—the man who had been a mentor to him since his return— and his brothers. He would ask his brothers for help. He wanted to get Sara away from danger, wanted to be back in the city himself, back in his own element. Once the sandstorm passed, tracking the bandits would be impossible, all signs of them erased. He would have to use other avenues to investigate.

Omar and all his manpower and wealth were probably working on finding Husam already.

The tire tracks came from the west and disappeared into a partially completed building that would be a hotel someday, fashioned after a famous medieval palace that had stood along one of the caravan routes many hundreds of years ago. Tariq preferred modern architecture like his company headquarters, but the resort had been designed to please tourists and fulfill their expectations.

Clenching his teeth, he kept his eyes fixed on the ground. It looked as if a number of trucks had passed in and out during the last couple of days. Any earlier and winds would have swept away the tracks by now. This was the season for sandstorms.

Tariq entered the building carefully. Only the first two floors were standing, nothing but the load-bearing walls. He checked around, but didn't find anything beyond some trash and cigarette butts. A gust of wind rose and pushed against him as he came out and strode across the sand.

"I got all the empty bottles," Sara said as he walked in with the pot of water. "We can fill them up for the road."

He nodded. In the desert, water was always the first thought—and the last.

"And I got everything that would burn," she added. "In case we need to start a fire. I found a lighter."

He listened to the desert for a few seconds, not liking what he heard. The winds heading for them were strong. "We'll probably stay the night." There was plenty of scrap wood around the construction site, and what she'd gathered would make perfect kindling.

She deposited her load in a corner, then gestured toward the door. "So what happened here? Why was this place abandoned?" She brought the bottles to him.

"Put on hold," he corrected. He wasn't the type to give up on something he'd started. Although some said his years of living abroad had washed the Bedu blood from his veins, apparently, enough remained. He would not give up the fight. "Permits were recalled."

Suddenly, and without any explanation, about three months ago. Just like everything else he'd tried to do, this project had met an impenetrable wall. He had a hard time getting new businesses off the ground. And even MMPOIL, which tens of thousands of his people depended on for survival, was regularly sabotaged. Tariq had managed to keep the company together only with sheer will and unending vigilance.

He didn't want to think that Omar had been right

when he'd opposed the new projects. Tariq had put it down to the old man's age. But perhaps Omar knew the country better and was more realistic.

A pang of guilt pricked Tariq at how much he owed Omar. And now he had let his mentor down by losing his eldest son.

"Did you have a bad builder? You'd think people who worked for a sheik would pay attention. Why were the permits revoked?" Sara tilted her head, exposing her graceful, slim neck, an expanse of creamy skin.

"Politics. Who knows?"

Her blue eyes hardened. She probably knew something about corporate maneuvering.

Tariq could go back at any time to the life and the company he had left behind in Sacramento. He'd been a valued executive there. Their doors would always be open to him, they had said. Staying there would have been easier. Certainly safer. But his fate, his destiny awaited in the desert he barely knew, and with the people who treated him as a foreigner. People whom, nevertheless, he loved. He cared little about the danger to his life, only to the degree that it would affect those who worked for him, and depended on him for their own safety.

His men had been killed today, Husam taken. The bandits had meant to take Sara, too. That had to be a coincidence. They'd seen her and wanted her; what man wouldn't? He couldn't fathom her being in any way connected to them. But he couldn't let any option go unexamined.

"Is this your first trip to the Middle East?" He watched her closely as he unscrewed the caps.

"And likely the last," she said. "No offense."

He could detect no telltale sign of deceit in her gestures or her voice. She had clear, honest eyes. If someone wanted her kidnapped, it would have been so much easier to do from her hotel, at night when she was alone, rather than when she was with a convoy that included armed guards. And who would have known about them going by car instead of taking the chopper, anyhow?

He thought of something else. When he did make his call, he was definitely going to ask for the helicopter to be looked at for signs of tampering. Until he knew more about that, he would focus on their only clue so far: Husam.

Now that he thought of it… "Wouldn't it have been easier to kidnap Husam when he was on his way home from work, alone in his car?"

Sara drew up her eyebrows as she considered. "Anything had to be easier than an armed convoy," she said after a moment. "So what are we missing?"

He shook his head. Damned if he knew.

"Husam called someone before we left. He joined the convoy unexpectedly. Maybe he knew the bandits. Maybe he went with them willingly."

"Why? And why kill everyone?"

"They wanted to take me," she said with a pensive expression.

"I have no trouble believing that he found you attractive, but kidnapping you? He could have just asked you to dinner." Tariq had considered that himself, after he'd gotten off the elevator and she'd gone up to the helipad.

He hadn't worked closely with Husam, but from all signs, the man seemed a competent businessman, hardly given to such outrageous crimes as kidnapping a woman. He was Omar's son. Was it possible for the fruit to fall that far from the palm?

"Okay. Fine. I'm just trying to consider all the possibilities." She straightened her spine and glared at him.

He admired her strength. Shortly after the attack, she'd been out there in the burning sun, helping him dig the grave.

He held her gaze. "A weaker person would still be curled up somewhere in shock."

Her expression softened marginally at his compliment. "I want to make sure we do whatever it takes to get out of the desert. They are not going to get me," she said.

"No, indeed." He would see to that.

She gave him a tremulous smile that made something clench in his chest.

"I'm glad we have these." He filled the last few bottles. "If we left the water in the pot, it would evaporate in the heat, and get dirty in the meantime." Intermittent gusts of wind swirled sand in from outside. "Be careful if you go out. I saw some tire tracks."

"You think the bandits visit this place? Why isn't there any security here?" she asked with some alarm, moving to help when the last bottle wobbled and nearly tipped.

"There's not much of value that's movable." The heavy machinery had returned to Tihrin when it had become obvious that the obstacle his enemies had put in his path wasn't one that could be speedily removed. "The site is on tribal land, anyway." No one from the tribe would damage the property. The people were loyal to their sheik.

For the most. Tariq thought of the possibility of Husam's betrayal. He didn't want to believe that one of Omar's sons could be like that, but now that Sara had planted the thought in his head, he had a hard time dismissing it. Maybe he'd been too focused on fighting with his enemies in the government, and had overlooked the dogs that slinked around his own backyard, waiting to bite when his back was turned.

Leaving her to screw on the caps, he strode to the window to look out at the endless desert, which, instead of sheltering him, as it had done for countless generations of his ancestors, had haunted him throughout his life.

"No time to set up the satellite before the storm." Locating the two-hundred-pound piece of equipment then dragging it back onto the roof would take considerable effort. He glanced at Sara and found her squaring her slim shoulders.

"I still think you should call Sheik Abdullah as soon as we can. He should be able to protect us." She seemed confident of that, coming back to it once again.

Everyone always thought that the sheik could do everything. But he hadn't been able to protect his family, he hadn't been able to protect his people, and there was a good chance he wouldn't be able to protect her.

And that he regretted profoundly.

"I *am* the sheik," he said.

Chapter Four

"What sheik?" She stared at him dumbfounded. He didn't look like a sheik. The first time she'd seen him—that morning in his Western-cut suit, with his unaccented English—she'd thought he might be American.

"Tariq Abdullah."

Sheik Abdullah! Oh, God. "But— If you're the sheik, why didn't they take *you* to be ransomed? Why take Husam?"

He shrugged. "They had no way of knowing I would be coming along. Could be they didn't recognize me in the heat of the battle. They had a goal and they were focused on that." He glanced toward the main entrance. "I'm going to make sure you get on a flight out of here as soon as possible."

Outside, the wind was swirling the sand.

"The bandits took my passport," she said, dazed. In novels, sheiks usually carried the soon-to-be-ravished heroines to their royal tent. Here she was, at a grim construction site, sitting on a blanket made in China.

"Then you will be taken to the U.S. embassy. They'll handle everything." He looked out over the desert where the wind was picking up.

Sheik Abdullah. She took a deep breath and blew it out, wondering feverishly if she'd said anything to offend him so far. If she messed up the deal she'd come here for… She was thinking for a moment as if everything was business as usual. Then pain hit her in the solar plexus as she remembered Jeff, whom some protective instinct had pushed out of her mind, so she could function. Images flooded her brain—of blood-soaked sand—and the job and the contract became insignificant.

Jeff was gone. She was alive only because of Tariq. *Sheik* Tariq.

"Thank you for saving my life," she said. "Sheik."

He turned back to her, crooked his head and actually smiled. Not the full-blown thing—heaven knew they had little to smile about—but a self-deprecating stretch of masculine lips over gleaming white teeth. Her breath got stuck under her breastbone.

"I think, all things considered, calling me Tariq would be fine. I hope I haven't hurt you much while trying to help."

"Good choice, considering the alternative." She

could barely feel the bump at the back of her head. She didn't want to think about what would have become of her by now if the bandits had taken her.

Sheik Tariq Abdullah. She was going to need a few seconds to process that.

"You didn't tell me."

"At first I wasn't sure I could trust you."

"Understandable."

He was nothing like she had expected. She'd been resigned to not meeting Sheik Abdullah at all. He was famous for being reclusive, an astute businessman who managed his tribe's assets with little personal publicity. Supposedly, a person could be in a business relationship with one of his companies for years and never once see him.

As a man, Tariq went beyond a woman's wildest fantasies. He was perhaps the most physically appealing male she had ever met, although he was not handsome in a conventional way. She found the energy that radiated from him mesmerizing. His movements betrayed strength and confidence. But the whole sheik business… She had a hard time picturing that. Where were his camels and his flowing robes, his tents and his Bedouin tribesmen?

"Why didn't we go to your tribe's camp instead of here?" She would have felt safer with people around them, especially the sheik's desert warriors.

The look on his face was one of faint amusement. "Except for a few small groups, my tribe rarely camps anymore, unless on a hunting trip for sport. They live in towns and villages south of Tihrin."

A day ago, hearing that would have been a major disappointment to her romantic soul. At the moment, however, she had bigger things to worry about. Still, she couldn't let it go without a question. "There are no more Bedouin?" But she'd seen pictures in the tourist guides.

"Bedu. We call ourselves Bedu. Foreigners call us Bedouin. Some tribes still have nomadic groups. I don't know any tribes that live fully in the desert anymore. Mostly, they come and go." He watched her, raising a dark eyebrow. "This saddens you?"

Was she that transparent? "I suppose. Doesn't it sadden *you?*"

He shrugged. "I grew up in a palace in Tihrin, then was sent abroad. I never lived in the desert."

So much for her sheik-flying-over-the-sand-dunes-on-the-back-of-his-black-Arabian-stallion fantasies. But one word caught her attention. "Palace?"

The expression on his face hardened as he walked away from the window. "My father was the king. And after him, my half brother," he said. "We'd better secure this place before the storm hits. We don't have long. See what you can do in here.

I'll search outside for anything we might be able to use for protection."

Tariq was royalty? Sara knew that the term *sheik* meant prince or king, but also knew that it wasn't strictly that way in real life. The guy who sold carpets in a small store across from her hotel called himself Sheik Jumah. She'd figured Sheik Abdullah was a tribal chief. She had no idea he was the son of a king.

She was staring at Tariq, slack-jawed.

"Sara?"

"Yes?"

"You know, I was really starting to like you. Don't go all weird on me now."

He was starting to like her! She resisted some deeply buried teenage instinct to ask, *In what way?* "No problem."

He was starting to like her. Yeah, that went a long way toward settling her down. *Not.*

Maybe she could gather her thoughts and act nonchalant by the time he returned. He seemed to be aiming for the door, picking up the tire iron on his way.

"You must be related to the current king then," she said without meaning to, her thoughts rambling.

"The king is my cousin. My grandfather was a powerful king and he had many sons."

"What happened to your father and your half brother?" Did kings retire? She'd read up on the country's economics with a special eye toward the petroleum industry, but hadn't spent time on its history.

He stopped on the threshold, and she watched his face darken, his jaw tightening. "They were killed. Bad luck seems to be the only dependable companion for the men in my family. You could say we're cursed with it."

HE CAUGHT SIGHT of a shadowy, moving shape between buildings to his left as he stepped outside their shelter. Too small to be a man. Tariq squinted against the sun as he gripped the tire iron and moved closer, keeping undercover, ready to fight.

A hyena.

The animal watched him instead of running away, simply skirted him when he got closer. Tariq shouted and clapped. It growled at him, ribs sticking out under the shaggy fur. *Could be trouble yet.* They would definitely need that fire during the night. The villa didn't have a door, nothing to keep uninvited visitors out. And the hyena might not be their biggest problem. Tariq thought of the tire tracks in the sand as he moved on.

The mangy beast followed.

If there was to be a fight, he hoped to regain his

full strength before it happened. He hadn't lost a dangerous amount of blood, but enough to slow him down. He didn't like the feeling.

He shook the tire iron at the animal and considered throwing the heavy weapon, then thought better of it as the hyena snapped its powerful jaws at him. Leaving himself unarmed didn't seem smart.

Those jaws could crush his bones with laughable ease. They went along with the beast's superacidic stomach, which could digest his whole prey—fur, flesh, bones, down to the last split hoof. If hyenas had a life philosophy, it had to be along the lines of "*waste not, want not.*"

Sara would have to be told to stay inside.

Sara Reeves.

Tariq had had lovers—both innocent and worldly-wise. But he'd never experienced the instant connection and overpowering attraction he felt for her. From the first moment in that elevator…

He'd known who she was. He kept a close eye on what business was being conducted at MMPOIL each day. He hadn't meant to meet her—that had been fate. But once he did, he'd had to join her on the trip to the wells, had to be near her again. He'd been thinking about asking her and Jeff Myers to dinner that evening, just so he could spend time in her company.

He had her company now. But he regretted the circumstances, and wished more than anything to keep her safe. It would be best for her if she left the country. Which she was eager to do, no doubt.

First he would get her to the embassy, then mount an investigation. He *would* find Husam and learn what was going on. He *would* bring the murderers to justice. But when he was done with that, he would go and find Sara Reeves again.

He went back to the workers' trailers and broke open a few more locks, got all the blankets he could find, grabbing a box of nails, too. When he returned to Sara, she was standing at the window as if mesmerized by the darkening horizon to the east.

"Storm's almost here." He dropped his load onto the floor. "See if you can seal up the windows." He went to the area that would be the bathroom and started shoveling sand out of the sunken tub, got it empty in only a few minutes.

"What are you doing?" She pulled a blanket from the pile.

"We'll be stuck here for a while. And we could both use a bath." The pool-like tub was four times the size of an ordinary bathtub, designed to be luxurious. It would take him a number of trips, carrying water, but he should be able to fill it at least partially. Cleaning up would give them something to do while they waited out the storm. Her clothes were covered in dry blood, and his wound needed tending.

"Stay inside and keep this close." He carried the tire iron to her. "You can use this as a hammer. Or a weapon. There's a hyena somewhere outside."

Her eyes went wide.

"If it tries to come in, just give me a shout."

"Would it attack?"

"Probably not yet. Assessing us for now. It's a night hunter, and more likely to make a move then. I'll get the fire going as soon as I'm done with this."

He dumped whatever water was left in the pot into the pool, then went to get more. As he did, he heard the sound of hammering—Sara nailing blankets over the window holes in the walls. She was making good progress. He hoped to do the same. He figured they had fifteen minutes at most before the storm hit.

THE WIND HOWLED like a wild animal, trying to get into their firelit shelter. The doorway was blanketed off, the fire a safe distance inside, an opening in the ceiling for the not-yet-built staircase providing a way for the smoke to get out.

Tariq sat on the opposite side of the dividing wall from Sara and the bath. His back flat against the concrete, he stared ahead into the semidarkness.

The sandstorm had considerably dimmed the

sun. Whatever light got through the swirling sands was blocked by the blankets over the windows, and the planks of wood he'd nailed up on the windward side so the blankets wouldn't be blown off. On the other sides, the nails were sufficient to hold the fabric, which kept the fine sand out.

"Why were *you* going to the well?" she asked, hidden from sight by the wall. The sounds of water splashing made his imagination run wild.

"My youngest brother, Aziz, called. He said he had something important he wanted to talk to me about." And he hadn't been willing to say it over the phone. Did he know about the bandits? "I wanted to hear what he had to say," he said, telling Sara the partial truth. He had gone because of Aziz's call, but he could have gone in a separate car under separate guard. He hadn't. He had wanted to see more of the beautiful woman he'd met in the elevator.

"How many brothers do you have?"

"Just two. Twins. Five years younger."

"I thought a sheik would have his own private chopper."

"Aziz took it to the new well this morning." Tariq had been planning on using the other one. Whoever else needed it would have been simply delayed an hour while the helicopter flew him out, then came back in for another turn. But the corporate chopper had been out of commission, and he'd met Sara in the elevator and been told shortly after about the two Hummers going out. And so, drawn by her, he'd come along for the ride.

Not the only last-minute addition to the convoy, it seemed.

He thought about Husam, going over each and every time he'd seen the man the last few months, every word they had exchanged, every project Husam had been involved in. Had he ever mentioned enemies? Had Omar? Tariq couldn't recall any such instance, so he thought harder. But he still couldn't completely block out the sounds of water splashing on the other side of the wall.

It'd been a long while since he'd had time to think about a woman. And the customs of his country made things difficult in the extreme, anyway. Had he spent any time in the company of an unattached Beharrainian of the opposite sex, he would have been expected to marry her. He was sheik, his every movement closely watched.

He had considered marriage for the sake of his tribe. He was willing to make any sacrifice for his people, even that. Holding an elaborate wedding, experiencing the blessing of children… Would it have been enough to forge them together again, to make them accept him, think of him as one of their own at last?

Trouble was, *he* wasn't thinking of himself as

one of them—not always. His mother's choice to send him out of the country and save his life had also cut him off from his roots, a decision that had been made for him and later proved to be as much a curse as a blessing.

"I really needed this," Sara was saying from the other side of the wall.

Even over the wind's howling, he could hear when she stood and stepped out of the pool, the water splashing onto the tiles. His groin tightened and he cursed his body's inconvenient awareness of her. He drew a slow, controlled breath, then let it out.

"Okay. Your turn," she called out after a minute.

He pushed himself to his feet and tried to clear his head as he came around the wall. At the sight of her, he felt as if he'd been thrown from a camel, a blow he had experienced only once, as a child, but still vividly remembered. There was no air in his lungs, none in the room, it seemed.

She stood by her soiled, discarded clothes, facing away from him, wrapped in nothing but a blanket. And still she looked as regal as an Egyptian queen, her wet hair tumbling down her shoulders to the middle of her back. The luxurious amount of it took him by surprise; she'd kept it hidden in a simple chignon before.

The light of the flames danced along her skin, playing on the drops of water on her shoulders.

She turned and caught his gaze, sensed his dangerous mood it seemed, because she stilled for a moment. The air thickened, as if the energy of the sandstorm that raged around them had filtered through the walls and filled the room.

Then she broke away and hurried around him to the other side of the wall, giving him a wide berth.

For a few seconds, Tariq simply stood there, breathing hard. Then he stripped off his clothes, wincing as he pulled at his shirt. The blood had dried, the silk stuck to the wound.

He hadn't realized how tired he was until he slid into the water, sinking in up to his neck.

The water that had been clear after her bath was now a murky red. He washed the wound first, then held that arm out as he cleaned the rest of his body.

They'd shared a bath. The intimacy of that didn't escape him.

When he was done, he pulled the plug and stood. Reaching for the five-gallon pot of water he had left for her, which she hadn't used, he dumped most of it over his head, rinsing away the last of the blood and dirt before he stepped out.

His clothes were too filthy to put back on, as were hers. When the storm abated he would bring more water, so the garments could be washed. He picked up a blanket from the floor and ripped it in half, wrapping one piece around his waist.

"You may come back."

She didn't do so immediately, and when she did, she looked nervous, tucking her blanket tightly. Did she think the scrap of fabric would keep him from her if he… Tariq shook off the thought, turned away. He wasn't a sheik of old who would throw a woman onto the back of his camel, then ride off into the desert and ravish her as he pleased. More's the pity. His heritage had never seemed as appealing as it did at this moment.

"How long is the storm going to last?" she asked.

"Hard to say." He turned back and drank in her beauty. "It could blow for a couple of hours or a couple of days." And he would be content to stare at her for as long or longer.

But she blanched at his last words, before pulling herself together with visible effort. Her gaze, which she'd carefully kept on his face until now, dipped lower. "Do you want me to look at your wound?"

He wasn't concerned about his injury. And the two of them in close proximity didn't seem like the smartest idea. But she was moving toward him already, and despite his better judgment, he nodded.

"The bullet went through." He'd checked after the attack, right after making sure she was all right.

She knelt next to him, close enough so he could smell the scent of her skin.

"You need some serious disinfectants and stitching," she said.

He looked at her. "You have medical training?"

She gave him an embarrassed half grin that made it impossible to look away from her mouth. "No, but we have a lot of medical TV shows in the States."

He grinned back. "I remember."

She lifted a hand to his arm, but held back at the last second, leaving her fingers hovering over his skin.

Heat swirled between them. Intensified. He held her gaze as the smiles slid off both their faces. Neither could deny the elemental force that had leaped to life.

Insane.

He had known her for a day.

But none of that mattered, no logic, no reasoning.

He leaned forward and watched her eyes go wide. But something from the outside penetrated the fog in his mind, and he paused, registering a lull in the storm. There was another noise, however, the rattle of engines. Trucks. At least two. He closed his eyes, and tried to judge their distance by the sound.

"WHAT IS IT?" Sara asked, reeling from the sudden heat and sexual tension between them.

Tariq had almost kissed her.

She had almost let him!

She drew back and pulled the blanket tighter around herself. What had she been thinking? This was completely unlike her. She wasn't the type to be carried away with passion. She thought too much, analyzed too much, and according to Jeff, she was too cold and measured.

Who was this woman, half-naked and contemplating heavy-duty lip-locking with a sheik? He did have amazing lips. Her gaze fell on them.

"Somebody is coming," he said.

That sobered her fast. "Help?"

He was a picture of alertness as he listened, his muscles taut, his body poised for fight already. Firelight glinted off his wide chest and flat abdomen. "I wouldn't count on it."

"The bandits?" Fear swept everything else from her mind.

Tariq shrugged.

She got up and hurried for her clothes, knowing they offered only the flimsiest protection, but wanting them still. The wind picked up again and howled as it rushed between the buildings.

"We should be okay until the storm is over," he said. "They can't see us. They can't see anything."

She slowed. He was probably right. The one time she'd looked out through a gap in the blankets, there had been zero visibility. "How did they find the place? Chance?"

"GPS."

She picked up her blood-soaked shirt with disgust, glanced at the dozen or so bottles of water they had. "Mind if I use some of that?"

"Go ahead. We can fill up after the storm."

She poured the contents of three into the pot. She shook the sand out of her skirt and jacket, and did spot cleaning on them first, getting the bloodstains out as best she could. When she was done, she soaked her shirt and his in the bucket. The murky water turned instantly red.

His blood. It was a miracle that he was still standing.

"How badly does your arm hurt?"

"It'll be fine by morning." He showed no concern for his injury, no sign of weakness.

She still found his intensity unnerving, but his obvious strength was a source of comfort.

"Let those soak for a while. We'll rinse them later. It shouldn't take long to dry them by the fire." He nodded toward the "laundry."

He was right, but she needed the distraction, wasn't ready to return to the blanket, to him.

"You should rest," she said. They would need all their strength and then some come morning, if the trucks they'd heard were the smugglers. "We'll take turns keeping watch."

His eyebrows slid upward as he gave her an

amused smile. And she pressed her lips together, realizing what she had said and the way she'd said it. He was a sheik. He probably wasn't used to being told what to do. But to her surprise, he didn't object.

"Come here." His voice was low and dangerous.

Against her better judgment, she obeyed.

"You first," he said, when she reached the blanket.

And since he was sitting on the far corner of it, she felt safe enough to lie down on the very edge with her back to him, careful to keep her covering tight around her. His nearness generated plenty of heat between them, but the temperature was dropping outside. The desert cooled rapidly at night, and their fire wasn't nearly substantial enough to heat a building as large as the villa. Goose bumps rose on her skin.

He must have been watching her closely, because the next moment he was by her side, running a hand down her arm.

"You're cold." He didn't wait for confirmation, but lay behind her and took her into his arms.

It seemed too fast by half, and way too forward. They barely knew each other. And yet they had looked death in the eye together and had survived, which had formed an undeniable bond. Then there was the irrefutable attraction, deeper and fiercer than she had ever experienced before, bewildering in its intensity.

The muscles of his chest felt solid against her back, his skin warm.

She needed to think of something, to start a conversation that would take her mind off that fact.

"Do your brothers and sisters work in the family business like you?" he asked, before she had a chance to speak.

Had he been searching for a distraction, as well?

"I'm an only child." To her father's great regret. He had wanted a large family to build a legacy. Toward the end, he had hoped that she would give him that, that the marriage with Jeff would result in a bushel of children who would grow the family business into a great success eventually. The superstores that had sprung up around the country were his inspiration.

She had stayed with Jeff longer than she should have because of her father's dream.

"Jeff was supposed to help you run the business," Tariq said, as if he could read her thoughts.

"I don't need help running it," she replied with more heat than she'd meant to. The subject was a hot button for her.

She had worked in the business since she'd been a teenager, was one of the best in her class at college and throughout earning her MBA. She had fought for and landed a highly competitive internship, and had proved herself with flying colors.

And yet her father had worried what would become of her and the company when he was no longer around.

He had been so relieved when she'd met Jeff and he'd expressed an interest in the company. She wondered now if she'd unconsciously tuned out the warning voices in her head and glided over some issues with Jeff. She had so desperately wanted to make the man who had raised her happy. They had dreamed big dreams together. She *was* going to make them come true.

She turned to Tariq. "I'm proud of what we achieved so far. And I can handle the company on my own." She wanted him to have no doubt about that.

"I didn't say you couldn't." He watched her thoughtfully for a few seconds. "What happened with the wedding plans? Without meaning to speak ill of the dead…Jeff Myers was never strong enough of a man for you."

Tariq was right, and it annoyed her that what he'd been able to see at a glimpse had taken her so long to grasp. "Enough time passed for me to realize that we didn't really mesh outside the office."

While her father had been alive, Jeff had deferred to him, but after his death, he took it for granted that he would assume full leadership of the business that Sara had helped build from the ground up.

"We didn't have the same goals." Jeff had thought they should go after profits more ruthlessly. Sara wanted to keep in line with the original mission statement, which declared support for non-fuel uses of oil, and education of the public about them.

"What are your goals?" Tariq asked.

"I want the company to stay the way my father and I dreamed it. I want it to make a difference. I want it to be something I can be proud of, something my grandchildren can be proud of."

He didn't respond, and she wondered in the ensuing silence whether he was pondering his own, much larger conglomerate. "What do you want out of MMPOIL?" she asked.

"I want to provide security to my people, and to preserve the Bedu code of honor while doing it. We need the oil, but I won't sell off our lands. I won't let oil extraction, or development, kill the desert, where we came from. I won't sell out to foreign investors."

It occurred to her as she listened what an enormous weight that must be on his shoulders—the well-being of his people. The hundred or so employees whose livelihood depended on her own company didn't come close in comparison.

"You should go to sleep," Tariq said. "You'll need your strength in the morning."

He was right. She turned away from him. Sleep would be good, just so she could forget about his nearness for a while. It couldn't be smart for the two of them to be lying like this, pressed together.

"What if you fall asleep, too?" she asked, dismayed at how throaty her voice sounded.

"Unlikely," he murmured, so close his hot breath fanned her neck.

He wrapped a strand of her hair around one long finger.

Okay—sharing body heat she could write down to doing whatever they could for the sake of survival. This she could not. And yet she couldn't pull away. Her body refused to.

"Look, I'm not the affair-on-every-business-trip type," she said, not daring to turn around.

"I'd hope not. But you feel this." It wasn't a question.

"We've both been traumatized. We're tired," she said, unwilling to acknowledge the attraction out loud.

"You think it's too fast."

"Yes."

He thought on that for a second. "Among my people, a bride might see her groom only once before the wedding."

"And you think that's normal?"

"No. Yes. For some people. I didn't grow up here."

"You said you lived in the U.S."

"From age five to thirty-five."

Which explained his flawless English. "So you're practically an American." She turned to look at him, curious about his life, about what had taken him from his country at such an early age, and what had brought him back.

She wasn't sure she could live here. But she was a woman, and their circumstances were vastly different. He was a sheik. She drew a slow breath, still not used to that thought.

"Don't let the civilized veneer fool you. America might have rubbed off on me. But it's nothing more than frosting on one of those cupcakes that are so popular over there. Beneath that, I'm Bedu."

Looking into his dark, glittering eyes, she had no trouble believing that. But the image… She bit back a smile.

"You don't believe me?"

"I do. I just wouldn't compare you to a cupcake." She grinned, then grew serious as her gaze fell to his chiseled chest and the shadows dancing on his tanned skin. He was a businessman, as cultured and competent as any she had met. But she'd seen him fight. Under his tailor-made suit he was a warrior.

"Then what am I?" He arched an eyebrow and watched her soberly.

She thought for a moment. "A mountain lion."

He seemed to be pleased with that. "And you?"

Right now, under his intense gaze, she felt like a deer caught in headlights. She couldn't tell him that.

"You're a lioness. We are the same," he said, when she took too long to answer.

And then he leaned forward and kissed her.

His lips were warm and firm and imbued with some magical power that wiped her mind clean. The passion between them was palpable, the kind that up until now she hadn't been sure existed outside of her favorite books. Though they were practically strangers, the chemistry they shared had a force of its own that made the raging sandstorm seem puny by comparison. She felt picked up and swept away, drowning in sensations that were impossible to resist, impossible to turn away from.

This was no tentative good-night kiss that might come at the end of a first date. This kiss was meant to brand a woman's soul. Tariq possessed her, instantly and completely. Heat pooled between her thighs when his tongue touched hers, even as she tried to resist his pull.

His long fingers caressed her hair, her face, her neck, dipping to the blanket and loosening it. Then his hand closed over her breast. Pleasure skittered through her, a thousand points of light.

She was so not going to do this. She had to stop. Now.

She kept kissing him and arched her back, pressing her distended nipple into the heat of his palm. He dragged his thumb over the sensitized tip, and she felt the shock down to her toes.

The deep, hungry growl that escaped his throat should have sobered her. She did pull away a little and look into his dark eyes, which gleamed with endless passion and heat. She could not glance away; she could not move back another inch. He held her enthralled.

With one long finger, he parted the blanket from top to bottom. She let him, mesmerized by the obvious need behind the soft fabric that covered his waist. Then he pushed her onto her back with one gentle hand and pressed closer, half covering her with his body.

Part of her said she was crazy for allowing this to go on. Another part insisted that she'd never felt this way before with any man, and what if she never would again?

He trailed his fingers between her breasts, over her stomach, to the cropped patch of hair below. Pleasure shot through her and had her trembling. Too fast. Too fast. The sensation scared her as much as it possessed her—frightened her *because* it possessed her.

She laid a hand on his chest and pressed against him. At this slight display of resistance, he stilled. When she drew her lips from his, he did not follow. But he leaned his forehead against hers, his breathing shallow and ragged, the first sign that he was as affected as she'd been. No, not the first. The hard proof of his desire pressed against her thigh.

She had come close to—

"We can't," she said, her voice weak.

"Why? What purpose would denying ourselves serve?"

"This is not how it works." She wished she could form a coherent thought. What was happening here? What she had nearly done, and some part of her was still contemplating… She wasn't like this at all.

"There are no one-night stands and quick hookups in the U.S.? That's not how I remember it."

She wondered how he had lived when he'd been there. A billionaire sheik. He'd probably had his choice of partners. And Sara was stupid beyond reason for allowing the thought to dismay her.

She pulled farther back, until they were no longer touching, until she could look into his dark eyes.

"I'm not a one-night stand sort of woman."

"Good. I'm not a one-night stand sort of man."

She retied the blanket around her. Tightly. And

was proud that her fingers trembled only a little. "I'm not going to do this." She marshaled the last of her willpower and resistance. "It's not going to happen."

The hyena laughed under their window, startling her back into his arms.

Chapter Five

Tariq crept through the night, sticking close to the buildings, staying deep in the shadows. Dawn had not yet arrived, but the moon lit their way. The storm had died down and their clothes were dry. Time to look around.

He couldn't sleep, anyway. Not after he'd touched Sara and experienced the depths of her passion, the sweetness of her mouth, the feel of her under him. She had drawn away. He'd pushed too fast, too hard. Found it difficult not to. His sudden and fierce need demanded he have her.

"This way," he murmured, and dashed across an open area, toward the large building near where he'd seen the tire tracks before. She ran behind him. Whoever had arrived in the middle of the night, in the middle of the storm, was most likely there.

Sara had come because they had but one weapon

between them, the tire iron, and they'd had to put out the fire now that the wind was no longer blowing. They couldn't risk someone smelling smoke. Tariq hadn't seen the hyena for a while, but he didn't want to leave her behind unprotected.

"Keep low," he whispered.

She ducked her head down, her hair tumbling around her shoulders. She hadn't put it back up. She was beautiful and sexy, with an incredibly hot body that made him ache with wanting. But there was so much more to her. Beauty alone couldn't distract him this much. The world was full of beautiful women, and there was no shortage of sexy bodies happy to press up against a sheik who owned a couple of oil wells.

He wasn't proud of the fact that in his youth he had taken advantage of that.

It'd been only over the last few years before he'd returned to Beharrain that the emptiness of his relationships had begun to bother him. And since he'd been here, he'd barely had a relationship at all.

Spending a day and a night with Sara Reeves made him wish for things he hadn't given much thought to before. And he couldn't afford to now. The task at hand required his full attention.

"Watch out." He pointed toward a scorpion that skittered across the ground a few inches from her feet. He kicked sand at it. The scorpion lifted its tail, but turned and moved off in the opposite direction.

Sara's lips tightened as she stared after it, but she didn't make a noise or any sudden movement that might betray their presence. "Poisonous?" she whispered.

"Yes." At the beginning of construction they had done an extensive relocation project, capturing scorpions and transporting them to the Rub al-Khali, the Empty Quarter, the uninhabited part of the desert.

Out of the dozens of species of scorpions in his country, only a few were poisonous. None had been found when they had surveyed the area, then shortly after work began, contractors came across several nests of them. It made Tariq wonder if they'd been brought in, yet another insidious form of sabotage. But as with the rest, nobody talked, nothing could be proved.

He moved forward again, creeping along the wall when they reached the building they'd been heading for. Sara came up close behind him the next time he stopped to listen for noises inside, their bodies separated by only an inch or two. He was aware of every soft breath she took, her every move, and wondered if she was as acutely aware of him as he was of her.

Back in the villa, she had pulled away. Probably

the smart thing to do—not that he'd liked it. The instant connection between them had probably taken her off guard as much as it had him. So he would give her time. As much as he could. He would plan a slow seduction. It hardly seemed possible, and yet he must, because he wasn't ready to walk away from her. He wanted more. A lot more. As soon as they were both safe and away from danger.

He moved on to the next window hole and glanced inside. "Two trucks," he whispered.

She stiffened, probably thinking about the attack. But she drew her back straight in the next second, and he knew if it came to that, she would be ready to fight.

"Not the same ones," he told her.

The trucks stood in the shelter of the walls, the one closest to him a Russian-made Kamaz. He couldn't see enough of the other one to identify it, but they didn't look like the beat-up military trucks that had attacked them on the way to the well. These were later models, in better shape.

Men slept, some snoring, on the sand that covered the floor.

"A single sentry," he whispered as he watched a youth of maybe twenty sitting facing the entry. His back was propped against the wall, and his head bobbed as he fought sleep.

Tariq focused on the trucks. "I want to see what

they are transporting." It might provide the clue to why his convoy had been attacked, why his oasis project was regularly visited by people who had no business being here.

"Be careful," Sara said.

With her on his heels, he ducked to keep out of sight, then rounded the building to get to the other side. Coming in the front would have been too conspicuous. But the structure had plenty of gaps in the walls. The best point of entry was a window hole on the other side, where the trucks would keep him out of sight of the guard.

Suddenly, the hair prickled at Tariq's nape. He wasn't consciously aware that he'd heard something, but he must have, because all of a sudden he knew without a doubt that they were no longer alone. He held up a warning hand for Sara as he stopped midstride and looked around slowly. A small sound came from behind a pile of bricks a few yards away. He flattened Sara against the wall and stepped in front of her, keeping the tire iron ready.

A shadow stretched forward in the moonlight. Was somebody crouching there? Tariq prepared to lunge. But then the shadow moved again and separated from the brick pile. The hyena. The animal growled at them.

Sara grabbed on to his shirt from behind.

"Keep still," he whispered.

"Over there," she whispered back.

He glanced around and spotted another, much larger shape between two buildings.

A camel? "How did that get here?"

Got lost in the sandstorm, most likely. Or it could be here with its rider, hiding out from the storm as Sara and he were, although Tariq would have expected the animal to be tied up in that case. Camels were notorious for wandering off, not something someone whose survival depended on the beast was likely to forget.

Encouraged by Tariq's attention being drawn elsewhere, the hyena crept closer. Tariq tried to shoo the damn thing toward the camel, but of course, the hyena was interested in him and Sara, smaller targets that would make easier prey. It eyed Tariq with a leer, not looking particularly impressed by the tire iron. Understandable, when its powerful jaws could easily snap in half the wrist that held it.

Tariq swung the length of metal, anyway. The hyena danced back, but didn't run away. And they couldn't shout, couldn't throw anything at it, couldn't make a noise. Tariq strode forward, keeping his body between Sara and the beast.

When he reached the next window hole, he looked in and took stock of the men inside from this different point of view. There were about two dozen of them, all sound asleep, apparently. But going in through this opening was still too risky. Tariq ducked down again and kept moving, turning back every few steps to keep track of the hyena, and of Sara.

When he reached the window he'd been aiming for, he looked inside and searched the dim interior carefully. Everyone in his line of vision seemed asleep. The trucks blocked his view of the guard.

He turned and handed Sara the tire iron. "Over there," he mouthed, pointing to a nearby stack of bricks that towered over their heads. He helped her up on top, trying not to get too distracted touching her. He kept his hand on her arm for a long moment, then reluctantly pulled away.

She would be safe here, out of the hyena's reach and out of sight if any of the smugglers wandered outside. Plus, from her higher position, she had a good view of the surrounding area, and could keep an eye out for anyone approaching. He stepped back to the window and leaned into the building, checking to make sure he wouldn't be stepping on anyone when he climbed in.

"Don't take any chances." The soft whisper came from behind him.

He nodded without looking back.

Silently, he pulled himself up to the sill. Then he lowered himself to the floor inside. His shoes sank a good inch into the loose sand that had been recently blown in by the winds.

The only light came from the moon peeking through many holes in the walls. Tariq had no trouble blending into the shadows. He walked slowly, in a crouch, and stopped frequently. A man who lay on the floor spread-eagle, snoring up a storm. The grating sound stopped just as Tariq passed. He froze. But a glance back showed the man still sleeping, his head turned in the opposite direction.

Crossing the ten yards from the window to the nearest truck took nearly as many minutes. Tariq lifted the corner of the canvas and looked inside. Too dark to see anything. He listened for sounds of breathing. Nothing. Not that he had expected to find anyone. No sense in sleeping in the stifling air of a closed, hard truck bed when one could sleep on the soft sand outside.

He pulled himself up and crawled in, letting the flap close, and complete darkness envelop him. He went by feel, bumping into wooden crates that filled most of the truck, leaving enough room for only a handful of armed men to guard the cargo when they were on the road.

Guns was Tariq's first thought. He wedged his fingertips under the top of the nearest crate, but had trouble prying it open. Whoever had closed it had nailed it down well. He searched around for a tool, but found nothing. Then he came across a banged-up license plate and used that. Precious minutes ticked by as he eased the top open a millimeter at a time. He froze when someone spoke in Arabic directly outside.

"Ready?"

A groan came in response.

Tariq ducked behind a crate so they wouldn't immediately see him if anyone checked inside. He felt around for a weapon, but his fingers met only crates and more crates. Fortunately, there was no further conversation, only footsteps walking away.

Probably the changing of the guard.

Tariq didn't dare move for a good fifteen minutes, until he could be reasonably sure that the guy who'd just come off duty was asleep. Then he lifted the crate's top and eased it off, reached inside. His fingers brushed against what could have been a bag of flour. He knew better.

Drugs.

On his tribal land. He gritted his teeth at the insult, at the danger that these smugglers were bringing to his people. This would be stopped, and he would be the man to stop it. As soon as he saw Sara Reeves to safety.

He inched back the way he had come and pushed the flap aside an inch, looked out to make sure the new guard wasn't anywhere nearby. But everything seemed the same as when he'd come in, with no movement among the men. Tariq went over the tailgate and dropped quietly to the sand, then crept to the cab and stepped up. Reaching in through the open window, he was grateful when he felt the satellite phone he'd dared to hope would be there.

He glanced at the men between him and the window hole in the wall, his way out.

He needed weapons, too.

But as he bent to reach for the AK-47 lying next to a bearded man on the sand, a shout came from the other side of the trucks, followed by sounds of people coming awake and jumping to their feet.

Tariq ducked under the vehicle.

Gunfire erupted at the building's front, and voices shouting and swearing angrily. He could see feet moving that way.

His heart leaped and banged against his rib cage. He tried, but couldn't see the source of the disturbance amid all the chaos. He only prayed it wasn't Sara. She wouldn't have left her safe position for anything, would she?

"YOU SHOULD HAVE STAYED out of it." The shah let his full disapproval sound in his voice.

His son hung his head with respect. "Yes, Father."

"And for what? A woman?"

"You have not seen her. She—"

"Silence!" he thundered. He'd had his share of foreign whores over the years. They had been a ready source of entertainment. That his son should become bewitched by one defied understanding. "Do you have need of another wife?"

"No, Father."

The boy had gotten the first at age seventeen, a fifteen-year-old, sweet virgin his mother had arranged for, and his grandfather had negotiated. The lad had been caught pestering the maids one time too many. Not that there was anything wrong with that; that's what they were there for. But should there be a child… The first son should be born in wedlock.

The shah scowled. He had no intention of letting history repeat itself. He'd acquired his son's second wife as a college graduation present, when the boy had professed to falling madly in love with one of his friend's sisters, at age twenty-two. The third wife had come just last year.

"Are you sure?"

"Yes, Father."

Good. The three wives the boy had so far were obedient, and had gifted him with many sons. Since the Quran allowed only four, the smart thing to do was to save the last one for when he was older, fifty or sixty or even more. A fourteen-year-old virgin could do miracles for a man's body and soul at that age, revitalizing him all over again.

"Go prepare yourself for the feast," he told the boy.

His closest allies would soon be here. He would reveal his secret to them. And then, with his son, his firstborn, his pride, together they would begin to reclaim their family's legacy.

SARA WAS LOST IN THOUGHT, trying to find some explanation for the out-of-character way she had acted with Tariq, feeling flushed all over again at the thought of his kisses and his hands on her, when the gunfire erupted.

Tariq.

She glanced around, but couldn't see anything from her perch on the brick pile. The hyena was nowhere in sight. After a split second of evaluating her situation, she slid to the ground. Had Tariq been discovered? He had to have been. Why else would the bandits be shooting?

She gripped the tire iron and peeked in the window. The trucks sat in the middle of the large open area. She could see men near the front of the building, but couldn't make out what they were doing, other than that they were upset over something.

The gunfire stopped.

Had Tariq been captured?

She waited to see if they would bring him back in, trying to think how she could possibly save him. What could she do against truckloads of bandits?

If he was still alive. She hadn't counted, but at least two or three dozen shots had been fired.

The thought of possible implications gripped her with icy fingers.

A dark shape separated from the deep shadow between the two trucks—a man hurrying toward her, keeping low.

Fear mingled with hope inside her. It could be that someone had spotted her, but it also could be Tariq. If it was one of the bandits, wouldn't he have shouted for the others? Hope grew even as she held the tire iron ready to swing.

Then the man reached the swatch of moonlight that came through the window, and she relaxed, stepping back as Tariq vaulted through the hole.

"Let's go."

Her wrist was caught in a band of steel that pulled her forward.

"Did they see you?" she whispered, hurrying to keep up with him.

"The hyena paid them a visit. I shouldn't have left you here." His voice was taut with intensity.

He picked a different path than the one they'd taken to get here, keeping in the cover of buildings and out of sight of the men, who were still milling about outside.

"Who are they?" she asked, struggling through the soft sand, which sucked at her feet with every step.

"Drug runners."

"How many?" She hadn't been able to see in the darkness.

"About two dozen. Well-armed." Instead of taking her back to the villa where they'd spent the night, he was walking toward the structure that housed the Hummer.

She glanced at the sky before they stepped inside. How long before morning? How much time did they have left in the relative safety of darkness? Couldn't be more than an hour or two. She tried to glance at his watch, but couldn't make out the dial.

"You think the bandits will find us once it's light outside?"

"They might." He let her go at last, and walked to the vehicle. "They could pile back on their trucks and drive out without ever looking around. Or they could be here for a couple of days, waiting for the handover of the drugs, if it's been arranged for this location. If they wander around, they'll see the trailer doors I busted. I think they come here often. They would notice the missing wood that we took for the windows. If that happens, they'll come looking for clues as to who was here."

She glanced at the Hummer. Even if the two of them could successfully hide, they couldn't hide the car. And if the smugglers took it... God, she didn't want to be stranded in the middle of the desert.

Tariq reached into his shirt, and only now did she notice the bulge there. She could have kissed him when he pulled out a satellite phone. Okay, she could have kissed him without much provocation at any time, but she was extremely relieved to see the phone.

He was dialing already. Then he spoke in rushed Arabic, before stopping to listen to the response from the other end. It couldn't have been good news. His face turned darker and darker, his free hand fisting at his side. He barked several questions, scowling fiercely as he hung up.

He set the phone on the Hummer's hood, then leaned against the car and rubbed his hands over his face. Then he swore. Heartily. In English.

When he was done, he looked at her and apologized.

"What is it?" Her heart clamored. Although she hadn't understood a word of the conversation, she knew something was seriously wrong.

"My brother Aziz was killed," he said. "The new well was blown up yesterday. Nobody survived."

"The well we were going to?" She felt light-headed and decided to sit down.

He nodded, a stony expression on his face. "The fires are still burning. Emergency crews are trying to put them out and cap the well again. My brother Karim is coming with a chopper. I told him where we are."

He picked up the tire iron he'd dropped as they'd come in, and she knew he was considering going back to fight those bandits, to find out if they knew anything about this, to take out his rage on someone.

But he wouldn't stand a chance. She needed to distract him until he calmed down a little. She couldn't begin to imagine what losing a sibling would feel like, but she had lost her mother at an early age, then more recently her father. She could understand the rage.

She stood and walked to him, placed a comforting hand over the one that held their sole weapon. "I'm sorry." She stepped closer and laid her head against his chest. She could hear his heart beating madly beneath her ear. "Were you close?"

He nodded, then began talking with some reluctance. "When I was a child in the U.S., I lived with distant relations of my mother. Their sons were older, and didn't much like the intruder they considered me. I spent a lot of time being ganged up on, or alone. I always thought of myself as the piece that didn't belong, fantasized about my real

family, how it would be when I returned. Perfect."
He gave a sour chuckle. "Then, after a while, I
grew up and forgot that I'd ever wanted to come
back. I suppose I was angry."

"At your family, for sending you away?"

"Yes. My mother said she wanted to save me
from danger, but she kept my twin brothers, who
were born just before I was exiled. Only they
didn't call it that. Everyone said I was going to
America to get a Western education. My father
had sons from other wives. He could afford to send
me far away to see if I learned anything useful to
bring back to him. As a child, I was often dejected.
Then over the years, teenage angst was added on
top of that, and I convinced myself I didn't care.
And later I made a life for myself separate from
my family."

"What brought you back?"

"A call for help." He drew a slow breath. "I
thought myself so separate from them, but a call
was all it took. My family and my people needed
me. They needed someone to take over the company, someone who knew how to lead a large business the Western way, who could negotiate on the
same level with the foreigners who poured into the
country to make investments. I had this fantasy that
everything would be perfect now. I'd be where I'd
always belonged. It didn't last long."

"This place is so different from the U.S." She could understand how someone who had lived decades away from it would have a hard time trying to fit back in.

"The same men who wanted me for my business skills didn't trust me, viewed me as a foreigner. I wasn't a perfect puzzle piece. I stood out. My own people didn't trust me, because I'd been away for so long. People outside the tribe didn't trust me, because I was half brother to the former king, Majid. The only thing that worked was my brothers."

"They accepted you."

"Without reservation. Despite the fact that, aside from a few brief visits, they didn't know me at all. We were strangers, but bound by blood, and that proved to be stronger than I could ever have imagined." Pain crept into his voice.

"You think this was an attack on your family?" He had told her other men among his relations had been killed before. In a subconscious gesture, she laid a hand on his forearm.

"It's possible." He dropped the tire iron and wrapped his arms tightly around her, buried his face in her hair. "I'm not going to let anything happen to you. I'm going to make sure that you're safe."

"Take me to safety then." Sara had a fair idea that

he had other plans—plans that would put his life at serious and immediate risk.

"Karim is coming for you. He'll make sure you get to the embassy and acquire new papers. He will guard you until you leave the country."

Tariq was going to stay and fight, do whatever it took to gain information about the attacks.

"Come with me." She drew back so she could look into his dark eyes, her heart aching at the raw pain in them.

"I cannot."

And she knew that no matter what she said, he wouldn't.

"Isn't Karim's coming here dangerous?" she asked. "The bandits have guns. They could take down a chopper."

"He'll pick you up two miles north of here. I'll take you there." Tariq pulled away reluctantly. "When I was out scouting yesterday, I found some oil they'd had on hand for the machinery during construction. I should be able to plug the hole in the oil pan and fill it up. Even if it leaks a little, we should be able to get to our rendez-vous point."

"And then you'll come back here?"

He nodded.

"What about the authorities?"

He opened the hood. "My half brother was not

a good king," he said darkly. "Half the people in the current government spent time in his infamous prisons. He didn't shy away from torturing political prisoners. People in power are not fond of my family. I don't trust the authorities."

"You're not your half brother," she said as he dropped down and crawled under the car.

He pulled himself out after a minute and searched around for several slivers of wood. He grabbed the tire iron, too. "The Tihrin chief of police lost his right leg in Majid's torture chambers. He is not going to do anyone in my family any favors," he said, back under the car again. His voice was filled with frustration.

He banged on something. Stopped.

"Do you have anything I can wrap around the iron so it'll make less noise?" he called.

She stripped off her suit coat and passed it to him. The muted sound was a lot quieter. Hopefully, it wouldn't carry as far as the smugglers.

He was done in a couple of minutes and crawled out, handing her back her jacket. Then he brought an earthenware jar filled with oil from the rear of the Hummer. When had he put that there? Probably when he'd been scouring the site for the satellite dish and carrying in water for their bath.

He filled up the oil pan, checked the level, then

closed the hood. "Let's get some water, then head out of here."

She moved toward the door, stopping to look around before she stepped out. No one was in sight, except the camel, which was licking a discarded brick about two hundred feet ahead. Nobody said camels were smart.

She and Tariq moved quickly between the buildings without talking. He was carrying the tire iron again. Dawn was breaching the horizon. As soon as daylight arrived and the bandits could look around the construction sight, they would notice the boarded up windows and come searching.

"I need to go back to the trucks," Tariq said once they were inside the villa. "I need a gun. I almost had it when the hyena came in, and then they were all awake, every gun in hand."

"You got out. Don't you think that's enough of a feat? You can get a gun from your brother."

"We'll need one before that. No matter how quietly we move, there's a chance that they'll hear. I want to be able to defend you. And if I could find a knife and slice their tires, they couldn't follow us at all."

And as an added bonus, the smugglers couldn't leave before he got back. That was part of his plan, too, no doubt. She stared at him, slack-jawed. "This is insane. You know that, right?"

"Most of them should be asleep again by now." He shrugged. "They came in late last night." He held her gaze, his mind obviously made up.

The only thing she could do was help. "What can I do?"

"Get the water to the Hummer and wait there. If anything goes wrong, drive north." He pointed to show her which direction he meant. "As fast as you can. Even if you miss the meeting point, Karim will find you from the air."

He meant if they killed him. Sara's blood ran cold at the thought.

"You'll make it," he said in a reassuring tone.

She didn't want to think about having to make it through the desert without him. She didn't want to think of him dead. He was little more than a stranger, but he had saved her life. And there was some undeniable connection between them, a zing of electricity that she couldn't begin to comprehend. She cared about him, felt as if she knew him, a lot more than she would have thought possible, given the short time they'd spent together. Of course, she'd seen him tested more than once, watched him endure incredible hardship. That had revealed his character and strength more than several months' worth of a casual relationship would have.

"Nothing is going to happen to you," she said.

"Not if I can help it." He came back to her and drew her into his arms. "I'm going to find you when this is over."

His head dipped slowly toward her. He was giving her plenty of time to pull away from the kiss. She rose to meet him instead. He didn't waste time with being tentative. He kissed her with full passion and need, taking her breath away.

Through the mist that obscured all coherent thought in her mind, three things became increasingly clear. One: Tariq was a man like no other she had ever met, and she wanted him more than she'd ever wanted another. Two: they would be lucky if either of them lived through this. And three: life was incredibly unfair. They could have met while he'd lived in California. She went to California on business all the time.

I will find you when this is over. Considering the kind of man he was, she believed that nothing but death could keep him from that promise. She clung to him, aware of the precarious nature of their situation, of the fact that he was injured, of the incredible odds.

She fisted her hands in his shirt and kissed him as if it was the last time they would be together. He kissed her back with the same desperate need.

And would have kept kissing him, but a small sound outside penetrated the haze of pleasure in her mind.

She froze.

Chapter Six

The sound came again. Tariq listened, reluctant to end the kiss. Probably just the hyena coming to try its luck again. The damn beast was nothing if not persistent. Tariq had the tire iron somewhere at their feet. He figured he had another second or two of savoring Sara before he had to pull away and chase the stupid animal off again.

But with Sara in his arms, he couldn't spare much thought for anything else. He wanted to protect her himself, and not trust her to Karim, even though he would trust his brother with his own life.

"Who the hell's been out here?" a heavily rasping voice said in Arabic, just outside the villa.

Sara froze in his arms. Tariq held his breath.

"Probably some camel herd. Better look around," another man grumbled.

They had about a second to hide. Tariq pushed Sara to the sand and draped a blanket over her, kicked sand over it, then dropped to the ground and wiggled in next to her. He barely had time to pull the satellite phone and the tire iron with him before the men came in.

SARA LAY WITHOUT MOVING, barely daring to breathe. Bandits scourged the villa, walking not a foot or two from them on occasion. If it weren't for Tariq's calm, solid presence next to her, and his restraining hand on her arm, she would have freaked out and betrayed herself a hundred times by now. She inhaled his masculine scent and soaked up the comfort of his strong, lean body, which he kept like a shield in front of her.

The men were talking excitedly in Arabic. She wanted to ask Tariq what they were saying, but would have to wait until they were alone again. The arm she was lying on went numb, but she didn't move. If anyone was looking their way, the slightest shifting of the blanket would betray that someone was hiding beneath. How long could they hold out?

Not long, it seemed. The following moment something hard connected with her shoulder. She didn't think she made a sound, but she must have, because someone yelled, a single shrill word. The next few seconds passed in a blur.

The blanket was lifted, and she saw two men. The one who must have kicked her in the shoulder was staring at her with a frightening grin on his dirt-smudged face.

Tariq rose with a roar, sand scattering all around him.

By the time she blinked most of the sand from her eyes, he had the guy who'd kicked her disabled. She could barely glance at him, where he lay on the ground with his head bashed in. Tariq, pipe held above his head, was running for the other man, ignoring the gun pointed at the middle of his wide chest.

"Run," he yelled to her.

He was never going to make it.

She lurched forward on instinct, knowing there was nothing she could do, knowing that as soon as Tariq was gunned down, she would be next.

But he threw the pipe, knocking the gun aside, then lunged at the man, flying through the air and landing heavily on his target. A mountain lion, indeed. He could have been an action movie stunt-man, except nobody yelled, "Cut!"

The men rolled on the sand, evenly matched. She hoped. How much would Tariq's injury slow him down? Was the other guy smart enough to notice it and use it to his advantage?

She dashed back to the dead man and snatched his weapon, aimed it at the other bandit's head as she moved toward him. "Stop!"

The men rolled, paying her no heed.

"Don't shoot," Tariq grunted as he flipped the guy again.

What did he mean, don't shoot? Of course she was going to shoot. Just as soon as her target stopped moving.

"Too loud," Tariq said on the next breath.

And she lowered the gun. He was right. It would be best if they kept quiet, so the rest of the bandits didn't come rushing to join the fray.

Great, so she couldn't use the gun. Okay, to be truthful, she wasn't sure if she would have been able to hit the right man, anyway. But she wasn't going to stand here, just hoping for the best. She tossed the gun out of reach of the men and looked around for a quieter weapon. The tire iron would have been perfect if they weren't right on top of it.

Her gaze landed on the heavy pot made of some sort of tarnished metal. She retrieved it, and when the men turned again so that the bandit was on top, she swung it, whacking him over the head with all her strength.

"I got him."

She didn't knock him out, but the unexpected attack stunned the man enough that Tariq could gain the upper hand. He got the man's knife from his belt somehow. He drew it up, and as they flipped, let his weight drive the blade home.

Both men went still the next second.

"Tariq?" She dropped the pot and rushed to untangle them. "Tariq!"

He sat up and looked at her, a quick grin spreading on his bruised but handsome face, though his dark eyes didn't smile. They looked tired, but alert, and something else she couldn't decipher.

"What is it?"

"You're lethal with a pot. I'd hate to see you with a cast-iron skillet." He pushed to his feet finally and retrieved the knife, wiping it on the bandit's shirt before shoving it into his belt. Then he collected the guns, handing her the smaller one. "It's time we got out of here."

He strode to the door and peered out. She followed. A few other bandits loitered around the water pipes. Maybe they wanted to get an early start. Maybe they were in a rush, meeting someone at a given time, wanting to make up for the hours the sandstorm had forced them to linger.

"You should be able to get to the Hummer without them seeing you. Keep to the cover of the buildings," he said. "Get in the car and stay down."

"And you?" Sand that still floated in the air from the storm dimmed the sun a little. Not enough to keep it dark, but giving the light an eerie cast.

"I'm still going to see if I can slice a few of their tires."

The idea just about stopped her heart. Was he insane? "There's no time for that now. They're awake," she said, with an edge of desperation in her voice.

His somber gaze held hers, telling her he was fully aware of the severity of the situation, and didn't like their options any better than she did. "We can't have them following. We'd never make it to the chopper. Go. If you run into trouble, start shooting. I'll come for you."

Of that, she had no doubt. But she would have preferred a plan that didn't include the use of any weapons. "Be careful."

"You, too. If I don't come for you, get in the car and drive as fast as you can." He held out his hand and pointed. "Karim will find you. If he doesn't, the closest village is a four-hour drive that way."

He held her gaze for so long that she thought he might draw her to him. She wished for it, for the feel of his strength around her, a moment of comfort. But both realized they had no time for anything except the quickest possible escape. He handed her the satellite phone, but kept the tire iron, stepped back and took off in the direction of the bandits, keeping low to the ground, hidden behind the chest-high rifts of sand the storm had created.

She started in the opposite direction, watching

out for bandits who might be searching through the site. How on earth was she supposed to get by them unseen?

HE HATED TO LEAVE HER alone, even if she *was* a fiercely independent woman. She was capable, he'd seen that. But she was in foreign territory. All the more reason for him to hurry and finish his mission, so he could get back to her.

Tariq cursed the dark shirt he wore, which would make him stand out from a distance. The bandits had camouflage uniforms made for the desert, the color of sand faded by the sun. He peeked around the corner of a building to judge how far it was to the next wall that would hide him.

Three men were smoking in the shade, about thirty feet away. They weren't looking in his direction, but as soon as he moved, they would see him. He waited a minute or two, hoping they would clear out. They showed no signs of getting ready to move on.

"Take another wife," the oldest of the men said.

"I have four already," another said as he stomped sand off his boots. "The law won't allow more."

"Divorce one," the third man advised with a sharp laugh. "It's easy enough."

"They all have children."

"Boys?"

"Mostly. Only two girls from the first."

There was a meaningful silence.

They were Beharrainian, their local accent unmistakable. Although most inhabitants of the Middle East and a large part of Africa spoke Arabic, the dialect changed from region to region, country to country.

Tariq didn't recognize the voices, and hoped the men weren't from his own tribe. But then again, he could hardly claim to know his tribe so well that he would recognize each voice. *Other sheiks would have.*

The thought pricked him with guilt.

Other sheiks lived their whole lives among their people. He'd been sent away at the age of five. Hardly his fault.

And yet everyone seemed to think so. Everyone expected more from him than he could deliver.

And four years after he had returned, as hard as he tried, he still didn't fully feel like one of them.

What man would betray the honor of his tribe by selling drugs that debased his own people? What kind of man would wait among sand dunes to shoot innocents, blow up oil wells that fed tens of thousands? What kind of man would throw aside the mother of his daughters? How was Tariq supposed to relate to that?

He knew well enough what would await a divorced woman—disgrace and poverty. If she was lucky and her father was still living, she might go back there. Or a brother might take her in. If not… The chance of finding another husband was slim. Most men here wouldn't dream of marrying anyone but a virgin.

Tariq winced, recalling the selection of sixteen- and seventeen-year-olds the tribal leaders had paraded before him, girls they'd expected him to marry to strengthen alliances. He might marry yet for the sake of his tribe, but by everything that was holy, if he did, he would wed a grown woman. Not one who had been forced into marriage by her male relatives.

His ideas did not make him popular among the conservatives.

He thought of Sara. If he had his way, if he were a man without obligations… He pushed the thought aside and drew back. The men didn't look like they were going anywhere. He would have to find a roundabout way.

He moved as fast as he could, the sand making it easy to proceed quietly. He rounded the next building and surveyed the area ahead of him. Nobody there. He dashed across the open stretch of sand and pressed against the unfinished wall of what one day would be a five-star spa.

"There'll be hell to pay." The words came from somewhere behind him.

The place was crawling with bandits.

He slipped inside the building and ducked down, making sure he kept under the windows as he moved toward the exit opposite. But a name caught his ear—Karim ibn Abdullah, his brother. Despite the heat, a chill nested in Tariq's chest. What had they done with him? He stilled.

"…the only one of the brothers left," a man said.

"He's a dark one," another responded in a glum voice. "He will want revenge."

"I'll take out his other eye and see if he can find us then." The first man laughed it off.

Karim had lost the sight in one eye in an unfortunate accident, at the same time as Aziz's leg had been crippled, twenty some years ago. Tariq had often wondered if the "accident" had been meant to kill them. It ended up saving their lives instead. Their father had declared them unfit to rule, and therefore no competition for his favorite son, Majid, who had eventually wrested control of the throne.

"The shah probably has plans for him already. We don't have to worry about him. Allah's will be done."

The other one grunted. "I wonder if all the money will be found when the brothers are gone, or if they will take their secret to the grave with them."

"The shah will find a way to get the treasure. I

wouldn't mind helping him." The man laughed. "He took care of Tariq and Aziz."

"I heard that those were accidents. He didn't even know Aziz would be at the well."

"He is a modest man. Doesn't like to brag…. So, do you still have that mistress in Khablad?"

Tariq moved along as the conversation switched to women. Grief for Aziz sat heavy in his heart. He clamped his jaw tight, fury coursing through his veins. Who in hell was "the shah?" Was Karim in danger? He had to get back to Sara and the satellite phone and warn his brother. But first, the trucks.

He walked through the building and stopped just inside the doorway. He was nearly at the vehicles. Unfortunately, more bandits hung around here.

He waited until one came near, then made a small noise. The man didn't seem to hear. Tariq kicked his boot against the wall. That stopped the guy. He turned toward the building and stuck his head in.

Tariq was ready. He'd considered the tire iron, but put a chokehold on the man instead, and with one quick move, pulled him in. A knife appeared, but he deflected it, then gained possession. Not that he could use the thing. Instead, he snapped the man's neck, then laid him on the ground and began to remove his uniform. A giant bloodstain on the cloth would draw attention, and he needed to blend in.

When he was dressed and had the white kaffiyeh wrapped loosely around his head—enough to obscure his features, but not so much that people would wonder what he was doing with it now that the winds had died down—he stepped outside.

Nobody seemed to pay attention to him as he made his way to the resort's main hotel tower, where the bandits were camped out. He slipped inside. Six men were visible, but he couldn't see into every corner. He walked about, keeping to the shadows until he made sure his first assessment was correct.

"Too early," someone said.

"We might have to stop again if there's another storm," a second man responded.

Tariq paid them little attention. He had a knife he was itching to sink into the tires, but three of the men were sitting near the trucks, sharing a carafe of Arabian spiced coffee. The scent of cinnamon carried in the air as one of them poured.

"…Gallbladder. I'll have to go into the hospital sooner or later."

"I hate doctors," his friend responded, and they began to swap horror stories of medical mishaps in their respective families.

Tariq scanned the blankets on the sand, packages of food, guns that had been left around, a five-gallon water jug. He pretended to go for water, and managed to swing an abandoned AK-47 over his shoulder in the process.

He moved toward the truck in the back, parked a few feet farther from the men than the one in front. He knelt out of sight, and was just raising the knife, hoping the hissing air wouldn't make too much noise, when someone came around the back of the vehicle, nearly falling over him. Tariq sprung up, one hand over the man's mouth even as the other was slicing his neck. He rolled the body under the truck, behind the large tire, where it might not be immediately seen. Then he slashed the rubber before moving on.

Four years ago, living in California, he would have found the idea of killing a man unthinkable. But a lot had happened since he had left that life behind. This was another world. Sometimes it seemed another reality, another dimension. He'd had to defend his life enough times that he'd learned to do so with skill. And when, in a disagreement over borders, a part of his tribe, his *fakhadh,* had clashed with a Yemeni gang that outnumbered them five to one, he had been expected to lead them in tribal warfare that seemed to throw him back centuries.

Except for the automatic weapons.

He didn't know whether to curse those or be grateful for their effectiveness, which had ended the fight in short order. In his great-grandfather's time, such an argument could have lasted generations before enough men were killed on each side that everyone felt honor had been restored.

The brief war had been a shock to his California, CEO sensibilities. But it had happened a few years ago. Now he was fully immersed in the volatile lifestyle of his countrymen. He was used to the fighting and the killing, the intricacies of Middle Eastern politics, the contrast of poverty and riches, the assassins. And he was getting used to being lonely, not being able to trust anyone.

Sara Reeves's clear blue eyes flashed into his mind. He could trust her, for now. She had little interest in his country, beyond the contract that had brought her here. A contract that was signed already and sitting on his desk back at his office, although she didn't know that.

Tariq crouched by another tire and sank his knife into it.

"How did this happen?"

"Who is responsible?"

People were coming back from scouring the construction site, talking with vehemence. He listened, then swore when he caught bits and pieces of the diatribe. Some bodies had been found. The bandits were organizing a search of the buildings.

He glanced toward the other truck, in plain sight

of the men. Couldn't reach it without being seen…
He had to get Sara out of here.

Unnoticed by the bandits who were milling
about up front, shouting and shaking their weapons,
he walked toward the other truck and stuck the
knife in one tire. But he couldn't do more without
risking discovery, so he headed out, regretfully
leaving behind the tire iron that had served him so
well until now. He couldn't afford to catch the
bandits' attention with anything that seemed out of
place.

He kept his head turned away from them, but
walked with brisk confidence, a man on a mission.

"You stay with the shipment," one of them
barked at him, apparently mistaking him for the
man whose clothes he wore.

"Be back in a minute," he said without slowing,
making his voice scratchy, as if something was
stuck in the back of his throat, or as if he'd just
woken up.

The man grabbed him by the arm.

If he tried to explain his way out of this, chances
were they would realize the voice wasn't right, nor
were the eyes. There weren't so many of them that
they wouldn't know each other. So he simply
turned and shrugged the man off with impatience.

He almost made it. It came down to a stupid bit
of chance, a coincidence. As the guy gestured in

displeasure, the barrel of his rifle got caught in Tariq's headdress and pulled it off.

Tariq had just enough time to register that the game was lost.

The next second a dozen guns were pointed at his head.

WHERE WAS HE?

"Come on, come on, come on," Sara whispered.

There was an awful lot of movement near the buildings, a lot of shouting. And the sounds were coming her way. She sat in the Hummer, expecting Tariq to come flying in so they could take off, but he didn't appear.

If anyone came up to the building before Tariq got here, he'd be sure to check out the vehicle. Under the circumstances, this didn't seem like the best place to hide. She got out, careful not to slam the door behind her, and looked around. No place to conceal herself here. She went to the back window. Bandits were running in and out of buildings, as if searching for something. It wouldn't be long before they reached her.

Fear and desperation coursed through her as she grabbed the gun Tariq had left her. Her other hand held the satellite phone. She would do what she had to, but facing the men head-on would be suicide. And the first one would reach her within seconds.

She tucked the gun and the phone into the waist-band of her suit—there was plenty of room, considering they'd barely eaten since yesterday—and rushed back to the car. Stepping up on the hood, she jumped and pulled herself up to the roof through a hole in the ceiling. At least, she tried to.

She was a businesswoman, one too busy to spend regular time at the gym. She bit her lip. It didn't seem this hard in the movies. Where was her upper body strength? Apparently, working on a keyboard all day long did nothing for her biceps. And her skirt wasn't helping, either. After a few seconds, it became abundantly clear why action flick heroines always wore pants.

Sara swung her legs and felt the gun slip, clenched her teeth with frustration. The only saving grace was that the weapon fell onto the sand instead of the car, making no noise at all. She swung harder on the next try and gained purchase with her feet at last, rolling away from the hole a fraction of a second before the first bandit rushed inside.

She held her breath, grateful that at least she still had the phone.

The man shouted for the others, who arrived in a hurry. She heard some banging. Were they kicking the car?

The engine started.

No, no, no. She and Tariq needed that to get out of the desert. What could she do? Distract the men until Tariq got there? What if he wasn't coming? She didn't want to consider that possibility. Lying low seemed to be the smartest thing for now. With some luck, they could get the car back once they regrouped.

Exhaust wafted up through the hole next to her. She fought not to cough.

Then the vehicle began to move, the sound changing as someone put it in gear and drove outside. They didn't go far before they stopped. She crawled toward the partially completed wall that would frame the upper floor of the building someday, hoping to get a glimpse of what was going on. Gunshots went off the next second, freezing her to the spot. At first she thought they might have seen her somehow, but no bullets pinged anywhere nearby.

Tariq?

Then an explosion shook the building, deafening her. She lay flat on her stomach. *Oh, God.*

Those bastards had blown up the Hummer. Why? What sense did that make? But of course, the idiots didn't need a reason. They were ticked off, and did whatever they damn well pleased. A peek over a low spot in the wall revealed a smoldering pile of twisted metal, confirming her worst fears.

Best case scenario—she and Tariq would manage to evade the bandits and survive. Yet they would still be stuck in the middle of the desert. Sara clung to the satellite phone, their only hope at this stage. The men were laughing as they strode back where they'd come from.

One of the trucks was rolling out of their headquarters. A couple of men jumped on, while others went inside. A few seconds later, two reappeared, dragging a man to the back of the truck. He was dressed like the others, but his wide shoulders seemed familiar. Tariq? Her heartbeat raced. She couldn't make out the man's bloody face. He seemed deathly still.

Fear and shock clutched her heart, and pain sliced into her chest. She waited for an eternity, her mind in turmoil, before the other truck appeared, as well. Then the bandits drove away. She waited some more, hoping Tariq would emerge from one of the buildings. When it became clear that he wouldn't, she went back to the hole.

They had taken her gun. She stared at the bare sand at least nine feet below her. No other way down but to jump.

If she broke a leg, she was as good as dead.

Not that she would survive all that long up here in the beating sun, without water. She stuck the phone in the back of her waistband and leaned forward to make sure she wouldn't fall on it. She would still be better off with a working phone and a broken leg than the other way around. She took a deep breath and jumped, yelping in pain when she landed hard on her feet and fell over, the shock reverberating up her shinbones.

She stood gingerly, testing her ankles. No major damage. She said a brief prayer of thanks as she limped to the door. The trucks were dark points in the distance.

She stared at the charred remains of the Hummer for a brief second, registering anew that she was trapped here. Then she flexed her ankles and started out in search of Tariq, scared of what she would find. The tension in her spine tightened with each empty building she walked through.

No sign of him anywhere.

Except for the bloodstain on the floor of the main building the bandits had slept in. They'd taken him. The realization was too scary to accept, but she couldn't deny it. She was his only hope. She needed to get with the program and make a plan. Where would they take him? She wouldn't allow herself to think that he might not be alive.

"Don't let him be hurt," she whispered into the empty air, fighting the desperation that threatened to engulf her. She was alone, without a car or a weapon. But she refused to think that all was lost. She had the phone.

Her fingers closed around it and she pulled it from her waistband, just as a dark shape appeared in the doorway.

Looked like she wasn't alone, after all. The hyena was here.

"Go away," she yelled, and glanced around desperately. She had nothing to defend herself with, so she grabbed a fistful of sand and threw that at the slobbering beast. That didn't seem to faze it. She drew a deep breath and tried to calm herself. Animals could smell fear. She raised herself to her full height, hoping to look more formidable. *Easy.* She could handle this. She had to, because she wasn't going to let Tariq die.

The repulsive scavenger meandered in, keeping its beady eyes on her, giving a bark. The sound reverberated across the room and bounced off the walls, sounding like deranged human laughter.

She stepped back, her heel striking something: the tire iron, half buried in the sand. Sara said a prayer of thanks as she used it to fend off the intruder.

Chapter Seven

The shah gripped his cell phone so hard the plastic squeaked in protest.

"You're sure it's him?"

"It is Sheik Abdullah. He said so himself."

The man had as many lives as a cat. The attack on the convoy had not been meant for him, hadn't been planned at all. The oilmen had been in the wrong place at the wrong time.

One of the men had recognized him after the fight, had thought him dead, but was too stupid to make sure. Had the sheik died, it would have been a bonus. But he seemed to have survived, after all, to interfere once again.

Was it a sign? Maybe Sheik Abdullah could be used for something. He was the king's cousin. No love lost there, but honor would demand that the monarch ransom him. For money or other advantages. It bore thinking about. And then there was the treasure.

The ex-king, Majid, Tariq's half brother, had amassed incredible wealth, not all of which had been found after his death. Speculation ran wild about where all the gold must be. Who would know better than Tariq, who had succeeded Majid as sheik of their tribe?

"Bring him to me," he said into the phone, before he flipped the lid closed. He didn't expect the shipment for another three days. They weren't far away, but there were no roads where they traveled, which slowed things considerably.

Sheik Abdullah. The shah grinned. Plenty of time to send for Abbas, who was an expert at getting men to talk. If Tariq knew anything about the gold, they would get it out of him. If it turned out he didn't, they could still ransom him to his cousin, the king.

SHE WAS INSANE. She belonged in a zoo along with the camel and the hyena. Preferably in a separate cage.

Sara held on for dear life as the camel she'd somehow managed to mount swayed under her, progressing forward with undulating movements. Why anyone would ever ride one of these beasts :d her. They were slow, stinky and uncomfortable in the extreme. And this one had spit on her! Had had to show his disapproval before they'd been able to come to terms.

Every inch of her skin was covered to keep the murderous rays of the sun at bay. Luckily, one of the saddlebags had been full of brand-new kaf-fiyehs, the traditional headdresses men wore. Maybe the animal's owner had been on his way to market.

She followed the tire tracks in the sand instead of taking the shortest way out of the desert. She couldn't leave Tariq.

He had saved her life. She wasn't the type who could turn her back on him now and live with that decision. The bandits had an hour's head start. She would follow and see where they took him. Once she had a location, she would call Karim again. He was searching the desert for them already, thanks to the satellite phone. She had called the last number dialed, as soon as she had managed to outwit the hyena.

Beharrain wasn't a huge country. The desert wasn't as endless as it seemed. Help would come; she had to believe that. And she would do whatever it took to survive until then. She glanced at the water jugs, at the blanket, the saddlebag where she'd stuffed the food Tariq had brought from the vending machines. Good thing that had been buried under sand, or the bandits would have taken everything.

She looked back and sighed. The hyena was following close behind. Probably waiting for her to fall out of the saddle. A distinct possibility.

"Go away!"

She had hoped to leave the beast in the proverbial dust, but the camel was so slow it would have lost in a race with a snail. *Race.* Didn't she read something in her guide book about camel races? Come to think of it, she was sure she'd seen camels on the National Geographic channel that moved faster than this one. So it *could* go faster. But how to make it?

She kicked the animal in the side gently. "Go!"

It ignored her.

She jiggled her body up and down in the saddle. "Go! Go! Go!"

The animal picked up speed. Marginally.

"Faster!" She slapped its side.

And to her surprise, the camel actually broke into a run. Time to hang on. If she thought her perch in the saddle had been precarious when the animal was walking, this was a hundred times worse. She needed all her skill and concentration to stay in place. She didn't dare turn and check on the hyena.

"Faster!" she yelled each time the camel thought about slowing, and the animal listened, responding to the tone of her voice.

She might have a chance to catch up with the bandits yet, depending on the camel's stamina. The trucks had been driving slowly when they'd left, probably due to the uneven terrain. The sandstorm had left drifting dunes behind.

An hour of galloping brought them to a rocky area, one that sloped upward, with mountains in the distance. Sara was fine while there was sand mixed in with the rocks, but once the rocks won out, she could no longer see any tracks.

The camel was slowing now, too, since the ground was harder to run on. It was probably tiring. She untied a new bottle—she had drained one already— and took a long drink, then glanced back. The hyena was a dot in the distance. But it still followed.

"Let's go." She urged the camel forward, scanning the mountainous region ahead. Then she noted movement on a ridge far ahead, and made out the silhouette of two trucks against the sky.

Maybe she could catch up a little before they completely disappeared. The camel could go through narrow passages that trucks couldn't. She gripped the reins with one hand, the saddle with the other, dark spots dancing before her eyes all of a sudden. She blinked them away.

The heat was strong enough now to kill. And there was little shade among the rocks, not even higher up the mountain. The sun was almost directly overhead.

She had two choices. To sit out the noon heat, hiding in the shade of the camel, letting that damn hyena catch up with her, and risk forever losing Tariq. Or to keep going, risking sunstroke and becoming hyena lunch, anyway.

"WHERE IS THE GOLD?" The man sitting by Tariq's prone body asked the question for the hundredth time, hissing the words through his yellow teeth.

Tariq closed his bloodshot eyes. Maybe he'd already died and was in hell. It seemed unlikely that pain such as this would exist anyplace but there. He turned his face from the blistering heat and blinding light of the flames next to them. Better. That spoke against hell. He didn't think a place like that would afford any relief.

The man kicked him. "Wake up and talk."

He opened his eyes and glared into his torturer's face, until the bastard turned toward the fire to pull out a stick that glowed red at the end. He lowered the hot tip to Tariq's exposed thigh, and there was nothing Tariq could do. He was bound tight, the man's foot holding his ankle to the ground. His pant leg had been ripped away a long time ago. Red welts lined his skin where he had been repeatedly burned.

"Where is the gold?"

Tariq turned his head toward the cave's opening, not wanting to see his flesh seared yet again. He clenched his teeth and stared out into the night. A sole sentry sat by the cave mouth, while sleeping smugglers lay scattered across the floor. They had gotten bored with his torture an hour ago, and gone to sleep, save the man who held the stick and seemed to have inexhaustible energy for causing him pain.

Fire branded his skin, but Tariq swallowed his groan, fought against the agony. He wasn't going to give the bastard the satisfaction of crying out loud. "There is no money." He said the words through gritted teeth, sweating profusely.

His torturer simply laughed and thrust the stick back into the fire.

Tariq kept his gaze on the small patch of sky and stars, trying to focus on them and on Sara's beautiful face alternately as the sickly smell of his own burned flesh filled the air.

Where was she now? There had been that explosion. And then the smugglers had taken him away, without him seeing Sara again. Had they killed her? Fear of that had tortured him during the long trek, and was more painful than the burns on his thigh.

What had become of Karim? Had he, too, been lost to a trap? Those thoughts bound Tariq more tightly than his ropes. He should have somehow defended Sara and warned his brother.

He watched as the guard at the mouth of the cave raised his head and peered into the darkness. Had he seen or heard something? Was Karim coming? Had he found them somehow? Tariq had been listening for the sound of a chopper, but hadn't heard it. Then again, torture did have a way of occupying a man's full attention.

The guard stood and walked away from the opening of the cave.

A shadow appeared a few seconds later and slid inside. Not the guard, and not Karim, either, but someone much more slightly built. He recognized the shape and swore silently in helpless desperation, even though knowing she was alive filled him with relief. She shouldn't be here.

He watched as Sara moved around, staying away from the area lit by the fire. He knew the exact moment she spotted him, knew when she decided to come out into the light to get to him.

His torturer was pulling the stick from the fire and giving him a demented grin, his focus fixed on his task.

Tariq could do nothing to stop Sara without bringing attention to her. Then she lifted something that in a split second he recognized as the tire iron. If they survived all this, he was going to frame it and hang it in the palace.

She brought the tire iron down hard on the back of the man's head, and he folded without a sound. Sara immediately dropped to the sand next to Tariq and covered herself with a blanket, in case anyone woke up and looked around.

"Sara," he said in a barely audible whisper, just to reaffirm that she really was alive and with him.

After a few moments, when no one raised the alarm, she reached out slowly, touched his face and left her hand there for a second. An amazing woman. He could only stare at her and drink in the sight. She was here, she was safe and she was about to save him.

She was already pulling water from somewhere and pouring it over his burns to cool them. She was an angel. *His angel,* he thought, with an urgent, possessive sense that took him by surprise.

He wished his hands were free so he could draw her into his arms. He inhaled a slow breath and held her troubled gaze in the light of the fire. "You shouldn't have come."

She was the one shaking her head now, even as she ran her fingers over the rope that bound him. "Karim is on his way."

Relief eased Tariq's tense muscles as she worked quickly, her movements impossibly quiet. He admired her temerity, her honor, that she would risk her life to save him instead of seeking to take the shortest route to safety.

"Thank you." Loyalty was not something he had experienced a lot of in his life, especially not over the last couple of years. Hers touched him deeply.

"Quick." He shifted as Sara worked the ropes

with nimble fingers. The tension in his chest eased with every millimeter the rope loosened. "You have the phone?"

She nodded.

Allah be blessed. They might make it out of here yet. He lay still, not wanting to make her job any more difficult.

She made no noise. He couldn't fathom how anyone could have heard her. But as he turned his head, he could see a dark shadow rise behind her, and before he could warn her, the butt of a rifle smashed hard against the back of her head. All he could do was roll forward, so that when she fell, it was on him instead of the rock floor of the cave.

SHE WAS BOUND hand and foot when she awoke. Bound to another person. *To Tariq,* she realized with considerable relief when she turned her head, the events of the previous night coming back to her. Sun poured in the cave's opening, and the men around them were going about their business. Nobody paid any attention to the prisoners.

She'd been captured. She had failed. Frustration and disappointment rose like bile in the back of her throat as she recalled her easy defeat hours before. She'd gotten knocked out briefly, and after she'd come to, she'd been too upset that they had caught her. It had taken her forever to calm down enough to fall asleep. She was tired still.

"Are you okay?" Tariq asked her, his voice low and gentle. His gaze burned into hers.

His strength and warmth comforted her. She nodded and wiggled her limbs to get some circulation back into places where the ropes cut off the flow of blood. Although she had managed to grab a few hours of sleep, she still felt exhausted and sore all over. "Where are we going?"

They hadn't been allowed to talk earlier, had earned some pretty hard kicks for every whispered word. But currently, nobody seemed to be paying attention to her.

"En route to some bandit camp."

"Still in Beharrain?" She remembered reading that the border between Beharrain and Yemen was fairly flexible in this corner of the desert, moving as the individual tribes moved with their animals from watering hole to watering hole.

He nodded.

She thought of the satellite phone, then remembered that the bandits had taken it after they'd knocked her out, along with the tire iron she'd been growing attached to. "What happened back at the oasis?"

"I slashed three tires before they discovered me. They had spares. And you?"

"Hid upstairs, caught the camel, then followed as fast as I could."

"You should have saved yourself."

"Right. I'm sure that's exactly what you would have done." She flashed him a skeptical look.

His split lips stretched into a pained smile. "Definitely a lioness." His gaze darkened and held her spellbound. "I've never met anyone quite like you," he said.

She grew embarrassed at the open admiration in his voice, not sure she really deserved it, and looked away. The uneven stone floor of the cave dug into her back, but she didn't dare sit up for fear of drawing attention to herself, to Tariq. They were lucky that for the moment they were forgotten. The bandits around them were finishing breakfast, some carrying their sleeping gear out of the cave, probably loading it back onto the truck.

"I think we'll be moving on." She scanned them one by one, mainly young men in their twenties. She could see only two or three who seemed older than that. They were all armed, an AK-47 hanging from each man's shoulder.

One of them yelled something in Arabic as he strode their way.

"What does he want?"

"They are ready to load us onto one of the trucks." Tariq sat up and helped her do the same. "Can you stand?"

She wobbled, but gave it her best shot. As soon

as the bandit reached them, she understood why
Tariq wanted to do as much as they could on their
own. The man was rough, gripping her much harder
than was necessary, his stubby fingers digging into
her flesh as he yanked her around.

Tariq said something to him in Arabic, a brief
sentence in a deep, harsh voice.

The man's eyes narrowed as he leveled his gun
at Tariq and shoved them forward. But he let go
of her arm.

They were at the cave's entrance, blinded by the
sunlight, barely able to see the beat-up Jeep that
pulled up to the level area on the hillside before
them. It came to a halt between the two trucks,
which had their engines idling.

A man in full tribal wear, including a soiled
headdress, got out. A moment passed before she
recognized him.

"Husam." The name slipped from her mouth,
and a cold shiver ran down her spine as the smugglers nodded to him respectfully.

Although he was too far away to have heard her,
the man's eyes zeroed in on her in the next second.

His face twisted into a frightful smile as he
strode toward them. "You are alive," he said to her
with a wide smile. "I had to come and see."

Tariq spoke rapidly and forcefully in Arabic,
lurching forward, but the man behind him held him

back. Husam sneered at him and pointed at her, switching to Arabic. One of the older men with the bandits came over, listened to Husam for a while. Tariq was still speaking, as well. She couldn't understand a word, but from the tone of his voice it sounded like he was alternately threatening and protesting.

The bandit leader shrugged and pulled a curved knife from the sheath on his belt. She shrunk back as he aimed it at her, but he ended up slicing the ropes that tied her to Tariq, instead of slicing into her, as she'd half expected.

Then Husam grabbed her arm, and the gleam in his beady dark eyes left little doubt about his intentions toward her. "I never wanted to do you harm. I meant to save your life. From the moment I saw you, I knew you were a gift." The look he gave her made it clear that he expected her gratitude.

"Let me go!" She struggled against him.

He seemed confused. "I'm offering you life." The smile was fading from his face at her resistance.

"You knew that the cars would be attacked."

"I knew our people would be in the same place that afternoon. I joined you to make sure you were spared." He sounded angry now at her lack of gratitude.

"Let me go."

"You will appreciate the honor of being chosen by me. You will respect me," he warned.

She tried to elbow him in his chest, but under-estimated the strength of his grip. He slowed his stride enough to backhand her, hard, across the face. She tasted blood and heard Tariq roar behind her.

Then so many things happened at once that she couldn't untangle the sequence of events, not even later, when she had time to think about it.

There came a number of shouts, then a sicken-ing thud, and Husam let go, falling face-first into the sand next to her, a dagger protruding from his back. Where had Tariq gotten that? At the same time, gunfire sounded, bullets slamming into the ground all around them. She sprinted forward on reflex, threw herself onto her stomach and slid under the Jeep for cover.

As soon as she was out of sight, she was out of mind, as well. Nobody came after her. Obviously, nobody considered her a threat. She watched with horror as the bandits focused on Tariq, who had drawn back into the cover of the cave, having somehow laid his hands on an AK-47.

The bandit leader and the young guy who'd brought them from the cave lay crumpled on the sand, and more bandits were falling by the second, Tariq's aim proving to be exceedingly accurate.

The rest of the bandits were lying flat on their stomachs among the rocks, some backing away toward the trucks. Then one appeared in the back of one of the vehicles, with a sinister looking weapon on his shoulder.

A handheld rocket launcher. She hadn't watched all those action flicks on late-night TV for nothing. The man aimed it straight at the cave's opening.

She rolled to the other side of the Jeep and came up to a crouch, slid behind the steering wheel. Nobody heard the motor rev over the din of gunfire. She floored the gas pedal and went after her target, who didn't notice her until too late.

He had time only for a horrified look as he turned the weapon on her. He couldn't fire, however. The next second the force of the collision knocked him clear off the truck bed.

Sara was stunned for a moment or two, having hit her head pretty hard on the steering wheel. Her vision clouded. She rubbed her eyes, the back of her hand coming away bloody. She reached up and touched her fingers to a gash in her forehead, brushed off shards of glass from the broken windshield. Then spotted the guy's rifle on the hood, which was crumpled under the truck's tailgate.

She stretched forward and grabbed the weapon

just as the man finally picked himself up from the ground—looking as stunned as she felt—and lunged for her. She pulled the trigger without thinking, feeling more surprise than anything when red bloomed on his camouflage shirt, and he crumpled to the ground, his eyes wide, his mouth open in a shout that got forever stuck in his throat.

She didn't have time to think about him.

She whipped back to the battle behind her and squeezed the trigger again. Moving the rifle back and forth in a sweeping motion, she pointed in the general direction of the bandits, her index finger frozen to the trigger until the last bullet was spent from the curved magazine, and for seconds after that.

When Tariq came up to her, with his arm bleeding again, but no sign of new injury, he had to pry the gun from her hands.

"Easy now. It's okay. It's over. You saved us." He drew her into his arms and held her as sobs broke free from someplace deep inside and shook her body.

She was a strong woman who prided herself on never falling apart, no matter the circumstances. Well, now she was falling apart spectacularly, and she didn't care. The events of the past few days, especially the past few minutes, had taxed her beyond bearing. If Tariq hadn't been holding her up, she would have fallen.

But he was holding her, his strong arms around

her, his lips on her hair, murmuring gentle words of encouragement.

She was sobbing.

"It's okay. It's over. I'm going to get you some water. Why don't you sit?" He was gentle and attentive, looking at her with concern.

"I thought we would die." Her voice sounded strangely weak. "But I—" She couldn't finish.

"I remember something my father told me after a battle when I was a child, although I didn't understand it then. He said for a warrior with a heart, the worst isn't the threat of dying, it's the taking of another life, no matter how unworthy the person is of living." Tariq rested his forehead against hers. "You are a warrior with a heart."

He overestimated her. She was no warrior, no lioness. She pulled away and sat on a rock ledge, watched him walk away after a moment. She'd managed to regain some measure of self-control by the time he returned, his bloody, shredded clothes replaced by a clean set of traditional pants and robe.

"We'd better get out of here." He handed her a heavy canteen, then bent to brush shards of glass from her hair while she drank.

"Somebody will come looking for Husam and the trucks sooner or later."

She handed back the canteen as she stood. They were in this together; she couldn't expect him to lead her around like some invalid. She drew a deep breath, filling her lungs. "What do you want me to do?"

"You could go back to the cave and rest while I pack for the road."

She shook her head.

"I didn't think so, but I had to try." He gave her a half smile. "Okay. You can gather supplies if you're up to it. Food, water, blankets, weapons. See if you can find that satellite phone they took from you."

She nodded and set off, her gait unstable at first before she found sure footing. As she walked around the carnage, she did her best not to look at the dead. Tariq was trying to back the Jeep away from the truck, but the motor wouldn't turn over.

"Can you fix it?" she shouted, before her attention was drawn to the rocks and the remains of a phone that had been reduced to slivers of black plastic. It had either met with a stray bullet or a hard-heeled boot during the fight. She lifted it and dangled some wires for Tariq to see. "I don't suppose this can be fixed."

He shook his head. "The engine looks busted, too."

"The trucks?" She nodded toward them.

"Probably equipped with locators. Their cargo would be worth over a million dollars on the open market. Whoever owns them isn't going to let them run around the desert without being able to keep track of his goods."

An otherworldly laugh sounded from some- where below them on the hillside. She started before she recognized it. "The hyena." It had followed her all this way. A shiver ran down her spine. "Are we stuck here?"

But Tariq nodded toward the camel, which was tied to a rock in the shade. The guard she had enticed outside with some odd sounds, so that she could sneak in, must have found it and led it there. She hadn't even noticed it until now.

"When you're done gathering supplies, why don't you give it some water to drink?" Tariq said. He grabbed the bandit closest to him and dragged the body into the cave, then the next, and the next. When he was done, he came for the camel and led it a good distance away. "Hold it here."

He walked back to the Jeep and came up with the rocket launcher, aiming toward the cave. The explosion blocked up the entrance, sealing in the dead.

Then he dropped that weapon and picked up an AK-47, heading down the hillside. "Stay here."

Soon, he was out of view of the ledge she was standing on. She heard the sound of a single shot, and a few minutes later Tariq reappeared. "If anything happens to me, I didn't want the hyena bothering you again."

He seemed winded. Odd for Tariq. She searched his face and noticed that he was paler than usual. Just how badly injured was he?

"Would you hold this?" She handed him the camel's reins, making sure to put them in his right hand. Not giving him a chance to protest, she reached for his other sleeve and ripped it to his shoulder, then gasped at the sight.

The bullet hole was infected, the welts an angry red, nearly black. He had to have a fever. She placed her hand against his forehead, and his fiery skin confirmed her suspicions. Sleeping against him, she had thought he'd felt hot because he'd been so close to the fire. But he was in much worse shape than he let show, probably walking by sheer will alone.

"How about your leg?" The thought of the merciless torture she had caught glimpses of when she'd found him sickened her.

"It's fine." He tried to hold his shirtsleeve together over his arm as he scowled at her.

"I should take a look."

"What's the point? There's nothing we can do about it right now."

They had a brief staring contest. Then he pulled up his loose pant leg. "We don't have time to argue about this."

She took in the half-dozen raw wounds on his tanned skin, the muscles in his thigh tightening as he bent to examine the damage. She could have wept for him. He had to be in pain, but nothing save the tight set of his lips showed it.

"Your brother will find us," she said, because they both needed hope, and she could offer no other encouragement. Tariq needed medical help.

"When did you talk to him last?"

"When I reached the cave. I described the hills to him."

"There are many hills here and hundreds of caves. They might have been setting a trap for him. I overheard them discussing him when I was going for the trucks yesterday."

"But I'd just talked to him."

Tariq glanced at the rocket launcher, and she knew what he was thinking. One of those could easily take a chopper out of the sky.

It would have been nice to catch a break somewhere. Just a single one. And who knew... She refused to give up hope. Which didn't mean she wasn't going to act as if they had nobody to count on but themselves.

She reached for the saddlebag on the camel and pulled out two headdresses. She wet one from the flask and wrapped it around Tariq's head, hoping to control his fever somewhat. The other she ripped into pieces, then wrapped around his wounds, once she'd washed them clean. Not nearly enough. He needed disinfectant, antibiotics and several stitches.

Frustration clamped her jaw tight as she stood and took the reins from him. She tugged on them, hard, until the camel knelt in the sand. Then she climbed up, making sure she would be in back, in case Tariq needed an arm around his waist to keep him from falling off.

He headed for the trucks first, however, and did something around the gas tanks. Soon both vehicles were engulfed in flames, along with their sinister cargo.

"We'd better go," he said as he hurried back. "Before they explode."

His robe fluttered behind him. In his traditional desert clothing, he looked a lot more like the sheiks of old than ever before.

"Where are we going?" she asked, when he slid into the saddle in front of her and took the reins.

"We are going to try and find the nomadic families of my tribe," he said, his voice not revealing weakness. But she caught a shiver that ran through him. "You are about to meet the Bedu."

They were several hundred feet away when the fire reached the gas tanks and twin explosions shook the air. If Karim was anywhere near, he would hear that, would see the smoke, which might act as a guide.

Of course, the same was true for their enemies.

She looked out at the endless hills to her left and the equally barren desert to her right. What were the chances that they would run across a small, wandering group of camel herders before their enemies found them, or before their water ran out? Or before Tariq fell unconscious from blood poisoning?

Chapter Eight

Tariq clung to life by sheer will alone, his head buzzing, his arm feeling as if it were on fire. His vision was dark and fuzzy, his ears popping.

"You okay?" he asked Sara, as he had done intermittently.

"Fine." She humored him. She probably knew there was nothing he could do if she weren't.

He wasn't going to find the Bedu. All he knew was the general direction of the places they camped. There weren't many areas where there was still enough grass to support the herds. He had pointed the camel that way and left the rest to Allah and luck, although it looked like both had deserted him.

"We'll stop soon." He hoped. The grazing grounds couldn't be too far off now.

If he couldn't get her to camp, at least he had to get Sara to a place where his tribe might find her, to one of the watering holes they regularly visited. Only one goal remained in his fevered mind—to save her. She could then warn his brother.

They were crossing a semiarid area that supported some vegetation, although sparse—a few scraggly bushes here and there, some yellowing grass. The breeze blew garbage around them, and he swore.

"What's wrong?" she asked, alarmed.

He gestured, his anger giving him extra strength. "People who dump their refuse in the desert. It chokes what few plants live here. When they die, the sand takes over. The desert becomes even hotter, with less rain. See?" He pointed. "We are in an indentation here. In the rainy season, water will gather and create a watering hole. The Bedu will come, unaware of the garbage rotting under it, and let their animals drink. There'll be disease."

She had her arms around him from behind, and now hugged him a little tighter. "When I researched MMPOIL's Web site, I saw that part about the desert preservation project."

"Yeah, that went over well." If he had any extra energy he would have laughed. "The Middle East is still a far cry from California, as far as environmental awareness goes." But he was working on it. He'd seen both good and bad things while he had lived in the U.S. He was working on bringing the former into his own country as much as he could.

They rode on silently for a while.

He was getting weaker as time passed, and hating it. Abandoning appearances, he finally let his body lean against the camel's hump, barely able to support himself. He needed to preserve what little strength he had left.

"Why did they torture you?" she asked.

"They think I have the previous king's gold, because I'm his half brother and sheik of the tribe."

"And you don't?"

"There is no gold. Majid amassed a fortune, but he wasted it as fast as he stole it. He spent insane amounts on luxuries, on building his army, on bribing people inside the country and out."

"So it's a myth?"

"It's becoming a legend. Even some people in our own tribe believe it. Majid used to hand money out to them to ensure their loyalty. They miss that. Some think I have access to vast treasures, and I'm just too greedy and want it for myself."

Loyalty disappeared faster than a drop of water in the desert when speculation about a secret hoard of gold bars and other treasures became the focus of conversation. That's why he saw Sara's loyalty as the true treasure and felt humbled that she would give it to him.

"But don't they see that you *don't* spend like the old king?" she was asking from behind him, her body pressed against his, her arms around his waist, anchoring him to the saddle.

"When I came back, I sold some of my family's assets and used the money to help my people, because they were in dire need. Some other well-to-do businessmen in the tribe didn't look favorably on this, probably thought that if I was helping, they might be expected to help, as well."

"They resented you for it."

"They figured if I had enough to hand out, then I must have whole fortunes. Then later, when I couldn't give any more without jeopardizing the businesses that are our future, they spread the rumor that I grew greedy and was keeping the rest."

"It's insane."

"And people outside the tribe believed the rumors very easily. Majid stole from them. They want to think that the money still exists someplace, and that they might someday get it back."

Tariq closed his eyes against the throbbing in his temples. "I receive at least a couple of petitions for restitution weekly. People hated me on sight for being Majid's half brother. He was the bloodiest king in recent history. Now they hate me even more, for supposedly keeping their money."

He clamped his mouth shut. He hadn't meant to let all his frustrations come out like that, but there was something about Sara that drew confidences, even from a man who didn't give his trust easily.

The horizon swam before his eyes.

He was fading fast. He had to do something.

He had to get the camel close enough to water so the animal could sense it and head there on its own. Camels could smell water from miles away, a trait developed over millennia of evolution. They were made for the desert. Tariq would take Sara as far as he could, then trust her to the dromedary.

"If I fall asleep, just follow the clouds," he said, doing his best not to sound as weak as he felt. He didn't want to worry her. Truth was, he was on the verge of passing out. His peripheral vision narrowed; the buzzing in his ears intensified….

"FOLLOW THE CLOUDS," Sara muttered to herself two hours later.

Great advice. Except that there *were* no stinking clouds!

Woozy from the sun, she'd let go of the reins a long time ago and given up any pretense of directing the camel. Instead, she concentrated on keeping Tariq in the saddle and forcing water between his lips at regular intervals.

Seeing him, a big, powerful man, defenseless like this was scary. She didn't want to think about the possibility of him not making it. She would get him to his tribe somehow. Even the nomads had cell phones and cars these days. They could take him to the nearest hospital.

She kept that in mind as she searched the skies. When she felt exhausted enough that she began worrying about falling asleep and tumbling from the saddle, she talked to keep herself awake.

"I was pretty young when my mom died. Sometimes her face flashes into my mind, clear as anything. But sometimes I can't remember what she looked like. I hate that. But I had a great dad. You would have liked him. You're a lot like him." Brave, strong, doing the right thing, focused on building a future, but never forgetting the people he was responsible for."

She went on talking about her family and the people at the company for a while.

"I'm addicted to romance novels and action flicks." She moved on to the next topic when she had exhausted the first. "I know some people think that's mindless entertainment. Their loss, as far as I'm concerned. It's not like being addicted to nicotine. I like happy endings." She wondered if this adventure was going to have one.

Heat radiated from above, as well as from the sand. It felt like noon in hell, but her sense of time said it probably wasn't even eleven yet.

An eternity seemed to pass before she spotted a

small gossamer cloud in the distance, sitting low in the sky. "Hey, they do exist," she muttered.

She didn't have to angle the camel toward it. The animal moved in that direction of its own volition, picking up speed. She held tighter to Tariq. If he fell out of the saddle, she didn't think she could get him back in. *If* the camel waited for them, which she doubted. The animal seemed pretty intent on reaching some invisible point on the horizon.

When she first made out the dark line on the sand, she thought it to be a Bedu camp. But as she got closer and closer, she saw green all around and no tents. Then the camel broke into a full trot without any urging from her, and soon she heard water.

"We're here. Wake up." She shook Tariq gently, but he didn't respond. She held him tight as she stared ahead.

The oasis that unfolded before her put her wildest fantasies to shame. She judged the island of green to be at least three acres, dotted with date palms. Several boulders towered at the far end, each twenty or thirty feet high, throwing some shade over the pool at their feet.

Heaven.

"Whoa. Stop. Sit." She yanked on the camel's rope, but the animal wouldn't stop until it reached water, until its head was submerged.

"We're going to get a drink, too," she said, on the off chance that Tariq could somehow hear her.

He was still alive; his chest rose and fell at regular intervals. She slid from the saddle—she couldn't get the camel to sit—and pulled Tariq down, but couldn't support his weight. The best she could do was break his fall. He didn't even groan as he hit the grass.

They had done a number on him, beaten him severely from the looks of it, in addition to his gunshot injuries and his burns. A weaker man would have allowed himself to slip away by now, just to escape the pain.

"I'm not going to let them win," she muttered as much to herself as to him. "They can all go to hell." Then she realized they already had. She was too worried about Tariq for that thought to make her feel any better.

The water was several degrees cooler than the air, shaded as it was by the boulders and palm trees. She rolled Tariq in, clothes and all, and went in after him to keep him from drowning. A good soaking couldn't hurt his sand-and-sweat-clogged wounds, and she had to bring his temperature down somehow. She dragged him farther in, gingerly, making sure the pool didn't deepen so suddenly that she lost her footing.

He was unconscious. If she let him slip to the bottom of the pool, he would drown.

"Hang in there. We're in the shade, we have water. The battle is half-won." She moved slowly, step by step, all the way to the base of the boulders, where the water seemed the coolest.

This was probably where the stream that fed it bubbled up from the ground.

She took off the headdress she'd worn and rinsed it with one hand, then draped it across her hair. She did the same with Tariq's, folding it and draping it across his forehead. Then she uncovered his injuries as gently as possible and washed his wounds.

He was in bad shape, the infection probably spreading through his blood. What was she supposed to do? He needed to go to the nearest E.R. But she couldn't do that for him. So she did the only thing she could: she prayed.

They were at an oasis. With water. Somebody would come here sooner or later. All she had to do was keep Tariq alive until then.

She stayed in the cool water for a good half hour before making for shore, and then only because she realized that she'd left the camel untethered, with nothing to stop it from wandering away. But the animal seemed content standing by the water's edge.

"Okay. Let's rest on the sand for a while." She floated Tariq's listless body to shore, pushed and pulled him to dry land and made him comfortable in the shade. Then she tied the camel to the nearest palm tree, close enough to the water to drink if it needed to. But it seemed filled up for now, and chose instead to go after the grass.

Sara's stomach growled. It'd been a while since she had regular meals.

She got a small bundle of food from the saddlebag, things she had collected from the bandits' belongings, and the remaining bags of chips and dried fruit from the vending machine. She unwrapped a package of dried figs and some white mess that smelled like it could have been goat cheese, or something else entirely, and was possibly spoiled.

"You have to wake up if you want to eat." She waved the cheese in front of Tariq's nose, using it like smelling salts in Victorian times.

He didn't react, and she didn't dare force solid food down his throat for fear that he would choke. She gave him water, and then she ate, not nearly enough, leaving more than half of the loot for when he came to.

Hopefully, that would be soon. If he didn't take nourishment, how was he to regain his strength and fight the infection?

The camel brayed, drawing her attention.

She'd assumed it was a male, based on its size.

What if it wasn't? If she could force some camel milk down Tariq's throat... She was on her feet before she finished the thought, kneeling by the animal and peering underneath its body.

Definitely male.

She blinked her eyes for a second in dismay, then shook off the unproductive emotion. She wasn't going to give up now. They were at an oasis. Somebody was going to come.

Tariq gave a low moan.

"Wake up. Come on." She hurried back to him and drew his head onto her lap, leaning against a palm tree, wiping his face with the damp head-dress. Their clothes were nearly dry already. She touched her palm against his forehead. It seemed the cold bath had lowered his fever a bit.

She would rest for a few moments, then repeat the procedure. There was little else she could do.

She must have dozed, because she woke to the sound of bells. And when she opened her eyes, confused and disoriented, she found herself surrounded by a gaggle of girls, who seemed to range in age from six to sixteen. They were staring at her with wide-eyed curiosity.

"Hello." Her voice sounded rusty as she looked around, hoping to see some adults, and at least a pickup truck. She didn't.

The girls drew back, the older ones pushing the

younger ones behind them. A herd of scraggly looking sheep drank from the pool at their back.

"I need help. Is there an adult around?" Sara scanned the water next, but couldn't see anyone else.

The tallest of the girls spoke rapidly in Arabic.

Sara pointed at Tariq. His condition needed no explanation. "Please."

The girl must have understood the desperation in her voice, if not the word, because she moved forward cautiously. She put a hand on Tariq's bloodstained sleeve.

Sara reached out slowly, doing her best to appear as nonthreatening as possible, and took the girl's hand gently. Tried, anyway. She drew back. Sara pointed to Tariq's forehead and placed her own hand there, then let it drop by her side. The girl understood at last and copied her, saying a single word. Probably telling her that Tariq had a fever.

Exactly. Now they were getting somewhere.

The girl spoke over her shoulder to the others. One ran off and came back a few minutes later with a wooden bowl with some white liquid in it. Sheep's milk? Sara held Tariq's head as the oldest of the girls took the bowl and little by little dribbled the life-giving liquid down Tariq's throat.

He choked and spluttered a couple of times, but got it all down.

"Medicine," Sara said, once he'd laid his head back in her lap. She drew aside the makeshift bandages and uncovered his gruesome wounds, then pointed toward the desert. "Help."

The girls were on foot. There had to be a camp or a village somewhere nearby. They had to have some medicine man, or a way to reach civilization.

"Phone?" she asked, and mimicked one, with her hand at her ear.

The girls looked at her, nonplussed.

They were all dressed in a mixture of clothing— traditional dresses, and odd items like sweatpants under them. She saw no sign of any sort of technology. If their family had a cell phone, it was most likely in their father's keeping.

"Go for help?" She pointed again, insistently, into the distance.

The oldest girl got up, but instead of running off toward the desert, she walked around the oasis, studying the ground, picking up blades of grass, and at one point stopping to dig up a white root with a stick. She washed her findings in the water, then came back to Tariq and picked up the empty bowl. She took a handful of grasses, chewed them to a pulp, then spat. She did the same with the root, bit by bit. When she was done, she mixed the disgusting paste with her finger, then scooped some back into her mouth for another round of chewing and spitting. By the time she was done, the end result resembled grits.

If she tried to feed that to Tariq, Sara thought, she might throw up from watching. But the girl set the bowl aside and pulled out a small, sharp-looking knife. She dug in her belt and came up with a Bic lighter that seemed oddly out of place in these surroundings. She held the blade in the flame.

When she was done, she pinched the darkened rim of Tariq's bullet wound and sliced it off with a clean, sudden movement that had Sara yelping. Fresh blood gushed forth. The girl mashed a handful of paste into the wound and it immediately seemed to stem the flow of blood. When that whole section of his arm was covered with the paste, she took the headdress and, with Sara's help, wrapped it tightly, like a bandage. Then she looked up and smiled.

"Thank you," Sara said. *"Shukran."* She used one of the half-dozen words she'd learned in anticipation of her trip. Then she inched up Tariq's pant leg and showed the girl his burns, pointing to the paste.

The girl shook her head and pulled a small vial from a leather cord around her neck, dropped a bit of the yellowish liquid it contained onto each burn. When she was done, she simply stood and took her bowl with her, disappearing among the sheep.

Another half hour passed before all the animals were watered. Then the strange group disappeared, swallowed up by the desert, nothing but a wooden bowl filled with sheep's milk proving that they'd ever been here.

Tariq seemed to be comfortably resting, but soon sweat beaded his forehead, and he began shivering.

Sara piled all the blankets on top of him, hoping this was the stage just before his fever broke and consciousness returned. She searched the desert, looking for help that she hoped the girls would send, but saw no sight of anyone, even though the sun was creeping lower and lower toward the horizon.

"Looks like we'll be spending the night here alone," she told Tariq. "You'll feel better soon, now that you've been treated. That Bedu girl really looked like she knew what she was doing."

He gave no sign that he'd heard her.

Sara considered pushing him up on the camel and trying to follow the tracks the small herd had left. But it would be dark soon, and she would no longer be able to see.

"Maybe we should have followed the girls." But at the time, she'd been certain that they would send help. And she likely couldn't get Tariq up in the saddle, anyway.

She wrapped the blankets tightly around him and fed him the last of the milk before she settled in for the night, lying awake for hours, sometimes talking to him.

She didn't know what time it was when she woke, but the sky was still dark and dotted with stars. She reached for Tariq's forehead and sent a relieved prayer of thanksgiving toward the heavens, which seemed within arm's reach here. His fever had broken. She drifted back to sleep.

The second time she woke the sun was breaching the horizon. She was lying next to Tariq, with him pressed against her back, his arms around her. She found his gaze on her when she turned.

"How do you feel?"

"Like I've been dragged across the desert by a racing camel, then tied to a hill of fire ants." Slowly, he pushed himself up to a sitting position. "I'm starving."

She brought him what food they had left. "It's all yours."

He ate sparingly. "We share."

"I already ate my half yesterday."

"We share," he repeated, giving her a look that said he wasn't going to budge on that point.

Her stomach growled, belying any protest she might have made.

"We had some visitors," she told him, as she

picked up a handful of dates. "Shepherd girls. They gave you milk, and one made some kind of poultice for your arm."

He touched his fingers to the bandages briefly. "Did she cut out the infection?"

Sara nodded, getting woozy just thinking about it.

"Tribal medicine is pretty effective," he said. "The king's brother married an American doctor who is obsessed with it. She's cataloging all the herbs and cures, and popularizing it all over again, so it won't be lost as the Bedu lifestyle disappears."

Having seen the miracle a handful of grass and an odd root did for Tariq, Sara could really appreciate that effort.

"Can you stand?"

"I think so." But he waited until he was finished with his meal. Then he pushed himself to his knees before trying to get to his feet. He was doing better than she expected, seeming only a little wobbly. "I'm going to take a dip in the water."

"You should probably keep your arm out." No sense in diluting the poultice or washing it away. The cure was obviously working.

"I might need help." His dark eyes glinted.

He couldn't possibly have the energy to think about mischief. "Believe it or not, we swam together already. I used the pool to bring down your fever."

He shook his head. "I don't remember."

"I'm not surprised."

"Thank you."

"No problem. Promise you won't do it again."

"Do what?" He gave her a brief smile.

Nearly die, she thought, but couldn't say the words. "Just promise you'll get us out of here."

"I promise. Come, the water is nice and cool."

She walked in fully clothed and moved toward him. The desert heat made it unnecessary to strip; their clothes would be dry minutes after they got out.

He was soon at the other end, where the pool was deepest, the water coming up to his shoulders. He leaned against the boulder behind him. "I needed this."

"Do you think the shepherd girls will send help?"

"Almost certainly," he said. "The Bedu have *diyafa,* a strict code about hospitality and helping strangers in need." He stepped away from the boulder and submerged all but his arm in the water, staying under for almost a minute before coming up again.

"Feeling better?"

"Stronger," he said. "The food did me good. The water is refreshing." He reached for her and drew her to him.

Sara went weak with relief that he had made it

through the night, that he was here and alive, talking, looking halfway healthy again.

"Thank you," he said somberly.

"We've covered that already." She smiled.

"You saved my life."

"I think we are pretty even on that score."

"Whatever you ask of me, it is yours. Within my power as sheik of my tribe," he added.

She wanted… She didn't dare voice what she wanted. She didn't dare admit it even to herself. Her wayward wishes were insane and unrealistic. "Actually, I pretty much like my life. I have everything I need."

His arms were loosely folded around her. Their lower bodies were nearly touching, their lips inches apart. She wasn't greedy for what he could offer her as a sheik, but she would have been lying if she said she wasn't interested in him as a man.

Her gaze settled on his masculine lips, and the memory of their last kiss came back with blinding heat. She swayed, chiding herself for the thought. He was wounded, and here she was, getting distracted by his body.

"Are you not well?" He sounded concerned. "Should we leave the water?"

She drew a deep breath. "I'm fine."

And then he leaned forward, slowly, and kissed her.

He tasted sweet, like the dried figs they had

shared. She kissed him back. Leaned against him. Then pulled away immediately. "Sorry."

He had a list of injuries. Had she hurt him?

But he tightened his arms around her and eased her back, claiming her lips once more.

She poured all her relief into the kiss, her wonder at the miracle that they were both alive. Then the tone changed between them, from a jubilant celebration of life to red-hot desire and sharp need. He commanded her body, her thoughts, leaving her lost and not wanting to be found.

What was it about this man that spoke to her like none other? From the first moment, she had felt the pull between them, and had been powerless against it. A part of her resented the feeling, since she liked to keep everything firmly in hand, especially her emotions. Another part of her reveled in it.

His hands slid to her waist, warm against her skin compared to the cool water. When they explored upward, coming around her breasts, she sucked in a gasp of air.

"Why does this keep happening?" she asked weakly.

"This what?"

"Us touching each other. This never happened with any other client. I had handsome clients before." She tilted her head back as he nibbled her neck. "Maybe it's the heat."

"Maybe we were meant for each other," he murmured.

Right. Because they had so much in common. She tried to come up with a solid rebuttal, but couldn't gather her thoughts just now.

"I want to make you mine in every way," he rasped against her mouth.

She nodded numbly, then got hold of reality for long enough to squeak out a not too convincing "No." She was breathing hard as she drew back. "You need time to heal."

"You could heal me," he said, and showed no sign of letting her go.

She wished she could heal him. For real, not the way he was thinking. "You have to save your strength."

"I find your nearness energizing. I find you..." His heated gaze caressed her face. "You're a surprise." He leaned forward and nuzzled her neck behind her ear.

No fair. That spot was extraordinarily sensitive. How was she supposed to keep a clear head and make sure they did the right thing for the both of them?

"You are too weak to do this. Just rest."

A part of him sprang against her. She wouldn't have thought he had enough blood left to get everywhere, but apparently whatever he did have was heading south. Typical guy. Freshly recovered from death's door and thinking of one thing already.

Not that she wasn't thinking the same. Maybe it was some built-in evolutionary response, celebrating life after a close call with death. His kisses alternated between gentle and passionate. She didn't think she had it in her to fight him. But as luck would have it, his arms loosened around her on their own the next second.

He was gazing over her shoulder. "Better get out of the water. Looks like we have visitors," he said.

Chapter Nine

He felt much weaker on dry land, where he had to support his full weight. In hindsight, his blinding desire to take Sara in the water might have been a tad optimistic. His body was a hundred percent better than the night before, but far from fully functioning.

Tariq watched the approaching dust cloud as he walked to the AK-47s leaning against a palm trunk and picked one up. "You should move into cover."

Sara stopped near a wider palm, pressing her still-swollen lips together. Her wet dress molded to her body, making him forget his injuries once more. But he couldn't ignore the approaching pickup. "You'd better wrap a blanket around yourself," he said, keeping his eye on the men.

Telling the good guys apart from the bad wasn't an easy task in the desert. A lot of the Bedu no longer wore traditional clothing, but dressed in army surplus camouflage suits. And they were always armed. Just because he saw AK-47s glinting on every shoulder didn't mean that the men weren't simple camel herders.

Which they turned out to be. He recognized one. Nawfal had come to him for a ruling on a dispute over a dowry. As sheik, Tariq was expected to decide cases brought to him by his tribesmen. He'd done the best he could, but was left with the vague feeling that he hadn't been able to please either the father of the bride or the groom.

The truck came to a halt twenty or so feet from him. He swung his weapon over his shoulder, but kept his hand casually at the ready. The last couple of years had pretty much erased the optimistic side of his nature.

"Assalamu alaikum." The men greeted him warmly, some falling to their knees on the sand with wonder on their faces. "You are alive. The sheik is alive."

"Walaikum assalam," he responded, more than a little bewildered by the unexpected joy they displayed, even uncomfortable to a degree at their deference. He wasn't used to that. At the corporate headquarters, Western norms of business ruled. At most, if someone really wanted to express respect or gratitude, he offered a slight bow of the head.

Nawfal stepped forward and exchanged the customary three kisses of greeting. The rest followed his example.

"When my daughter said there was a sick man

at the oasis, I did not realize it was you, Sheik Abdullah," he said. "Forgive our tardiness. Night fell by the time the girls returned home with the sheep. She told me she cared for you as she had learned from her mother, and that the stranger had his wife with him." He looked searchingly at Sara.

A logical assumption. In most countries in the region a man and woman traveling together had to be either married or related. Although Beharrain was more progressive than that, hoping to court the tourism industry, some outlying areas held fast to tradition.

"You couldn't have known. Sara Reeves is here from America on business. Her team and mine were killed. We were ambushed on the way to the new well."

Nawfal's face tightened with anger. Tariq might not have been a favorite as far as sheiks went, but such betrayal went against the Bedu code of honor. He bowed. "My life and the lives of my sons are yours."

The others repeated his declaration without hesitation. They were pledging to follow him into the fight when he went after his enemies.

Their response took him by surprise once again. He'd expected their support to be offered a lot more grudgingly, if at all. Had he been locked in his corporate offices so long that he'd misjudged his people? He had always thought that *they* misjudged *him.* But even so, would it be right to blame them if he'd never given them the chance to get to know him better?

"When news came that you'd disappeared, we thought you might have been killed at the explosion at the well. Will you honor us by coming to our camp?" Nawfal asked, his dark eyes glinting with hope and jubilation. Having the sheik as a guest in a man's tent was a high honor.

Tariq glanced at Sara. His first instinct was to commandeer the truck and drive them to Tihrin, return to his palace unseen and keep her safe there while he figured out the identity of the bandits' leader. If the girls had been able to walk back to camp last night, then the men could do so, as well.

But Nawfal's daughter had saved his life. Maybe it was time he stopped running from the desert. His enemies were here. He had to defeat them here. He looked at the men and found himself saying, "Yes. I thank you for your hospitality." But he wanted to talk to Karim nevertheless. "Do you have a phone?"

Nawfal pulled a cell phone from his pocket. "No good here."

Of course. And satellite phones, at over fifteen hundred American dollars apiece, were way too expensive for the average Bedu.

"My brother Karim might be in danger. Aziz was killed. Have you heard?"

The man nodded soberly, and the jubilant smiles slid off the faces of the others, as well. A few *insha'Allahs* were murmured.

"As soon as we reach camp, we'll send my oldest son to Tihrin to alert your brother. He is a good, strong man. He will carry your message."

"Let us go then." Tariq gestured toward the pickup. He translated the gist of the conversation for Sara, then drew up an eyebrow at the glint of curiosity in her eyes and obvious anticipation in her smile. He would have thought she would be eager to return to the city.

"I always wanted to see a Bedu camp," she said with a grin. She was no longer calling his people Bedouin.

"I would have thought the only thing you'd want to see was the airport as your flight takes off." The thought left every cell in him protesting.

She watched him with her beautiful blue eyes. "You don't think I'll be safe at the camp?"

"I'm not sure I can guarantee you'll be safe anywhere," he said ruefully. "All I can promise is that I'll protect you with my life and ask my men to do the same."

"If I go to Tihrin will you come with me?"

"If you wish. I will protect you."

"But you'd rather stay here."

"I want to talk to the people at the camp. They know the desert, know who comes and goes. I might be able to get information I couldn't gain anyplace else."

"A day or two at a Bedu camp isn't going to make a difference. I'll go back after that," she said.

Relief unfurled inside him. He wasn't ready to let her go. He wanted to get to know her better, wanted to find out what made her the remarkable woman she was. Not that an extra day or two would be enough for that. Or that he really believed he would be ready to let her go after so short an extension.

He pushed the thought aside. He would deal with that problem when he came to it.

The men were already piling into the back of the truck, leaving the cab for Sara and him. Probably none of them felt comfortable sitting that close to a foreign woman.

The back window of the truck was missing, so they could communicate without trouble. But Tariq didn't need to ask directions. He'd seen which way the men had come from, and the tracks in the sand were as easy to follow as road markers. An hour passed before he caught the first glimpse of the camp, black goat-hair tents stretching across a large, rocky plateau with enough soil to support some sparse vegetation. A small group of camels loitered to one side. He couldn't see the sheep herd Sara had told him about. The animals were probably grazing somewhere nearby.

Two more pickups stood by the tents, each as

beat-up as the one they were traveling in. Large plastic barrels filled the back of one, which he knew from experience to be water containers.

"Have you been here before?" Sara asked.

"Once." He had little time to travel around, but he'd made a point of visiting each camp shortly after he'd returned to Beharrain.

His people hadn't been impressed. After thirty years abroad, he'd spoken their language with an accent, an ever-present reminder that he was no longer one of them. That had disappeared by now, but he knew first impressions were exceedingly difficult to change.

He'd felt like a fish out of water, grateful to return to the city, to a corporate environment he was familiar with. And as time had passed, after all the hints that his people had lost faith in him, he'd been reluctant to face them again until he could show results. He'd thrown himself into his job with full force, working nearly around the clock.

Tariq wasn't expecting a warm reception now. So the feast they magically put together minutes after he'd arrived took him by surprise. Three sheep were roasting over open fire pits. He wondered if these families could afford such extravagance. His tribe was oil rich, but cash poor. They were paying enormous restitutions to other tribes, blood money and other debts left behind by his half brother, Majid.

Tariq sat with the men smoking the water pipe,

an acquired taste that he'd actually grown fond of. Once again, they expressed their relief over finding him alive.

His wound had been examined and dressed again by Nawfal's wife, the tribe's traditional healer, immediately upon his arrival. Nawfal's eldest son, a man of twenty, who was to marry within a week, had been sent to Karim.

Tariq had been presented with a traditional outfit that was clean and beautifully decorated. It had probably been Nawfal's groom suit upon his marriage, and carefully stored away ever since for special occasions. Tariq glanced around for Sara, but couldn't spot her. Hadn't seen her since they rode into camp and the women had whisked her away.

"So you know these men?" he asked the old grandfather seated across the fire from him. They were talking about the recent activity in the desert, convoys of trucks and the men who escorted them, armed to the teeth.

"Yes, my sheik." The old man looked at him with such hope in his eyes that Tariq had to glance away in embarrassment.

His people had apparently felt the absence of a leader keenly, and his sudden appearance made them hope that he would put an end to the comings and goings of the gangs of bandits insidiously infiltrating the region over the last year or so.

"Where do these bandits come from?"

"The south," the old man responded as he puffed on the pipe. "They take what they want—food, water, animals. They have no respect for their elders, and harass the women. We don't dare let our wives and daughters take the herds to the far grazing grounds anymore."

In traditional Bedu society, men saw to herding the camels, while women took care of the sheep and goats.

"Where are the smugglers going? Where do they take the drugs?" Tariq asked.

"Toward the western hills. They have caves there. The camps that way had to move. Can't graze up the hillsides anymore, either."

The others around the old man nodded.

"How many of them are there?"

"Hard to say," Nawfal stated. "We've seen a dozen different trucks at least, but there could be others that travel outside of our territory. It's always just a truck or two at a time, but they have bigger weapons than we do."

Tariq nodded, remembering the rocket launcher.

"You have not reported it," he said with some anger. This problem should have been taken care of long before it escalated to attacks on travelers and blown-up oil wells. Did his people not trust him to defend them? Did they think he had no honor, and would fail to protect his tribe? Or did they believe that he wasn't strong enough to accomplish the task?

"Three times we have sent a request for help," the old man said, with reproach in his eyes.

Looking into them, Tariq believed him. "I did not receive your message." One possible answer came readily to mind. "Husam ibn Ibrahim worked for our enemies."

The faces around him drew tight with anger. Betrayal was taken seriously among the Bedu.

"May Allah blacken the face of any such traitor," Nawfal said with heat.

The others nodded.

For a moment Tariq thought of his ancestors. Not his father, who'd been a weak-willed king at best, but of his grandfather and his great-grandfather before him, the founding sheiks of the country. Those men had taken on enemies, both foreign and internal, and forged a nation, creating prosperity for generations to come.

They were great men, true Bedu. And what was Tariq? He could scarcely claim to be like them, a warrior of old. But he was a man who deeply cared about the welfare of the people he was responsible for. And maybe that would be enough.

He sat up straighter and called on his ancestors' spirit of strength. "It is time we cleared our land."

The men drew forward, the excitement of battle glinting in their eyes, and maybe some newfound respect, too. Tariq set aside the pipe and began to rough out his newly hatched plan.

DARKNESS WAS FALLING by the time Karim arrived. The two brothers greeted each other warmly before Sara was introduced and, to her surprise, was invited to a strategic meeting in Nawfal's tent. "We must go on the offensive," Karim said.

They were speaking in English—for her sake, probably, Sara thought.

Nawfal was pouring spiced coffee. Tariq paced the tent. His traditional dress was amazing, fitting his wide shoulders to perfection and adding an air of untamed warrior to the man. But it was Tariq's brother, Karim, who drew Sara's attention, for she couldn't help comparing the two.

"We'll recruit a force," Karim continued.

Nawfal nodded. Tariq had told her that the man had already pledged his support.

Karim wore a black T-shirt and cargo pants with boots, looking more like a commando than a member of the sheik's family. He had a deeper tan than Tariq's, proving that he spent a lot more time in the desert. He was powerfully built, just like his older brother. But he was more brusque and less patient. He scowled a lot and made swift, forceful gestures as he talked.

His left eye was so intense that it bordered on scary. Nawfal tended to fall silent and look away every time that dark gaze landed on him. Karim's right eye didn't move at all. Nobody had said anything about it, but from watching him, she was pretty sure he was blind on that side.

A four-inch scar started above the eye socket and ran down his cheek, giving him the look of a fierce desert bandit. His impeccably polite manner toward her and his obvious care for Tariq were the only things that softened the image.

"It'd take too much time," Tariq said. "Right now, we suspect where they are. If word gets out that a crackdown is being prepared, they will disappear into the desert. We must go now, even if we have fewer men. We have the element of surprise on our side."

Karim still scowled, but nodded. "On my way to the city, I will circle the hills and get an exact location. In the morning, I'll return with our security force."

Tariq glanced at Sara. "You should go with him," he said. "He'll take you to Tihrin."

With the attention of all three men on her, she wished she had taken the time to bathe and change clothes when they had arrived at camp. She'd felt fine then, however, and too eager to follow the women around and see camp life to bother with that. She hadn't been dirty, had taken that swim with Tariq in the morning. Now, however, she was covered in grime from preparing for the feast. She'd even assisted the women with butchering the sheep, and that had been a messy business. Sure brought back memories of early childhood summers at her grandfather's cow ranch in Texas.

She smoothed her stained clothes. "I'd rather stay."

Tariq and Karim lifted dark eyebrows in identical expression of surprise.

"Karim has enough to do without having to see me settled first," she insisted. "I'll be safe here. I can return to Tihrin tomorrow after the fight." She hoped they were buying her excuses. The truth was, she wasn't prepared to leave Tariq this suddenly, with barely a chance to say goodbye. She was afraid that if she went now, she might never see him again.

She wanted another chance to talk with him, although she wasn't yet sure what she wanted to say.

Sara expected him to put up a fight and insist she go now, but he surprised her by simply nodding.

Karim raised his eyebrow even higher as he considered them, but didn't offer any comment. Instead, he took his leave so he might have a chance to survey the mountains by daylight.

Sara, too, left Nawfal's tent, and went in search of the women. One thought was uppermost in her mind—that she had just been granted another night with Tariq.

ABSOLUTELY ENCHANTED, Sara waited in the tent that had been lent to them for the night. The warm-hearted women had treated her like royalty. She'd been given a deep blue dress, richly embroidered and beaded, a headdress decorated with silver medals, and loose silk pants.

She was looking forward to shedding her grimy clothes and putting on the clean garments. The headdress she would wear only when she left the tent. The women had provided her with water for bathing, some fantastic herbal soap, and scented oil. Her skin was crackling dry from wind and sand.

She wiggled out of her shirt and set it aside, glancing toward the entrance of the tent. She'd been inside others, on invitation of the women, and had seen a divider hanging in the middle, usually an expertly made carpet. There was none here, save those on the floor, but pulling one up would have exposed the sand. The camp was situated on rocky ground, but it seemed the people had taken great care to clear the area under their tents, spreading a thick layer of sand for comfort, and carpets on top of that.

She appreciated the fine rugs underfoot, but some sort of barrier would have been nice to shield her from whoever might walk through the front flap. She looked around, her gaze settling on a length of silk that had no apparent purpose. Maybe nobody would mind if she borrowed that.

THEY WERE GIVEN Nawfal's son's new tent, which his family had prepared for him in anticipation of his wedding.

Tariq stood rooted to the carpet, staring dry-mouthed at the erotic play of shadows displayed on the silk. Sara had lit on oil lamp on her side against the approaching darkness, and was in the middle of her bath.

And baths being what they were in the desert, heaven help him.

The screen hid nothing, only softened her curves as she bent to the bowl at her feet and dipped in the large sponge, brought it up and slid it over her body. His own body's response was explosive and immediate.

He should have walked back out. He couldn't. He cleared his throat, figuring he should at least give her some warning that he had entered.

"I'm here." His voice was uneven, like that of a teenager going through puberty.

She jumped a little. "I'm just washing up. I'm almost done."

"I'll leave." Could he? He must.

"You don't have to." She abandoned her leisurely pace and washed with more vigor now. Her breasts bounced slightly as she ran the sponge over their globes. "What did you find out from the men?"

That conversation seemed like a million years ago. Tariq's mind was full of something else entirely at the moment. But he forced himself to think back and produce a coherent response.

"The bandits have been around for a while.

There are several dozen of them. Maybe as many as a hundred. They seem to be well armed."

"What's the plan?"

"Some of our men know where their main caves are. They are prepared to go and fight. They've had enough harassment. All they want is a leader."

She stilled. "You." She didn't sound happy.

"I'm sheik. I'm expected to be able to take care of the troubles of my tribe."

"Why not the law?"

"The bandits bought the law."

"Government troops, then."

"I doubt this government would rush to my help."

"You said that before. Are you sure?" She began moving again.

He swallowed hard. "My half brother killed the current king's father. He kidnapped the king's son and sisters. He did his best to kill the woman who is now queen. The current military is formed specifically of men who hated my half brother and volunteered their lives to try to stop him and take him out. I don't think they would do much for our family."

"Oh." Sara stopped again, turned slightly sideways, her perfect breasts clearly outlined.

His body hardened further, especially parts below the belt. "I am leaving. I'll come back later."

"Done." She stepped away from the bowl. "Just let me quickly put on some moisturizer. How do you feel?"

She didn't want to know. "I can see you," he admitted in a rasping voice.

Her hands flew up to cover herself in strategic places, then she changed her mind and bent to drag a handful of clothes in front of her.

He opened his mouth to apologize, but something else came out. "Don't," he pleaded.

They stood motionless, facing each other now. He could clearly make out the curve of her hips.

"You should have left with Karim," he said hoarsely. It would have been the sanest thing to do. He would never forgive himself if anything happened to her. But, by Allah, he hadn't been ready to let her go yet, wasn't sure if he ever would be. The fact that she had wanted to stay thrilled him and made him hope impossible things. "You shouldn't be here," he stated with his last remaining shred of sanity, then regretted it when she drew back.

"Sara, I— What I—" Damn it all. Sheiks did *not* stutter. "I'm glad that you're here. Too glad. It's not safe. If I were less selfish… There's something—"

She dropped whatever she'd been holding and stepped closer to the flimsy divider. "I know."

He drew a long breath, his nostrils flaring as he moved forward. Only inches divided them now, and a bit of translucent silk. He could see her, but she couldn't see him, since his side of the tent was dark.

He raised his hand. "Come closer."

She did, so close that her nipples brushed against the silk.

He kept his palms open as he ran his hands over her, heat diffusing in his body. "Closer."

Now her whole naked body was draped with gossamer silk, outlined, all of it. She was as beautiful as a piece of art, although Islam forbade the depiction of the human form. Hers stole his breath as he rubbed his thumbs over her hard nipples. Then he could not resist any longer, and bent his head to suck gently on one through the silk.

SHE'D BEEN AROUSED by his voice alone, by the knowledge that he was in the same tent with her while she was naked. The feel of the cool silk on her body and the heat of his mouth created an exquisite contrast, making heat and moisture gather at the V of her thighs, and the muscles in her legs weaken.

"Tariq." She was incapable of saying more than the single word.

His hands molded the thin fabric to her skin and roamed her body in a thorough exploration. She couldn't see him, could only feel him, leaving all her attention free to fully enjoy his intimate caresses.

Pleasure washed over her, but she wanted more. She wanted him to kiss her like he had kissed her that morning in the water.

"Tariq." This time, her voice pleaded with unspoken need.

He understood, and with one movement, pulled

the barrier from between them. Then his lips were pressed against hers. And she could hold him at last, wrap her arms around his strong, wide shoulders.

He claimed her mouth, his tongue imitating what her body desperately wished for. He tasted of spiced coffee. His lips worked hers with sure expertise, eliciting wave after wave of red-hot desire.

She could see him now, too, in the ceremonial tribal outfit, his dark hair glinting in the light of the lamp, his dark eyes glowing with untamed desire. He was more than the sheiks of her fantasies—more fierce, more proud, more passionate. And tantalizingly real.

"Tariq." This time, she spoke his name in unconditional surrender.

His hands slid under her buttocks and he gathered her close to him, let her feel his full arousal. She pressed against it. He lifted her, aligning her center with his. Hungry for more, she wrapped her legs around him.

Only when he was lowering her to the carpets did some semblance of sanity return.

"What's happening to us?" she asked when, for a moment, their lips separated. "What must your people think?" She was well aware that she was in a very traditional society.

"I would imagine they think you are my mistress. Some sheiks keep a number of them."

Mistress. She resented the word, the archaic idea. But wasn't that what she was heading toward? Becoming the sheik's mistress? She knew full well she couldn't be more. Their worlds were too different. Her life was back in the U.S., his was here.

"Stay with me tonight." His gaze was heated, his voice low, his warm breath fanning the side of her face. She knew exactly what he was asking.

She could feel the heat of his palms, feel his vibrating presence surrounding her. She could feel his need, and couldn't deny that there was a matching need burning within her.

She responded to this man like no other. They might have to part soon, but not yet. Not yet.

The strength of the connection between them, the scorching heat, didn't seem possible. They barely knew each other.

She'd told him that before, and he had said many happy marriages had been built on shorter acquaintances. And this wasn't about marriage. This was about one night. He would leave with his men to go after the bandits in the morning. Didn't she deserve a single night of reckless pleasure? Fate owed her a few hours of happiness after the men she'd had the bad luck to date in the past, after the years of loneliness.

She leaned into the heat of Tariq's body and kissed him.

NEED WAS DRIVING him mad, forcing him to go too fast. The iron control Tariq wanted was slipping through his fingers, fast. Sara was a treasure, a one-of-a-kind desert rose, the perfect drop of wild desert honey. He wanted to savor her. He wanted her taste on his tongue for the rest of his life. He never wanted to forget the feel of her under his hands, under his body.

His body, which at this moment did not know the meaning of savoring.

Not when her full breasts were pressed against his chest, and the scent of her skin invaded every brain cell he had.

He forced himself to glide his hands over her slowly, keep them on her lightly, to touch her gently with his mouth. It might have worked if she'd acted cool or reluctant or fragile. But she kissed him with the full power of a woman, with passion, her tongue sliding against his in silent imitation of what his body urgently demanded.

He tugged the scrap of silk that remained between them out of the way, his controlled passion making his fingers tremble. He was grateful for the semidarkness of the tent, where only a single oil lamp flickered. For the fact that her eyes were closed, so she wouldn't see just how much she had shaken him.

But her eyelids fluttered open, and she looked straight at him and smiled.

He became drunk on the passion in her blue eyes, which had darkened so much they looked black. He supported himself on one elbow next to her while his free hand brushed over her soft skin, toward her breasts, which captured his attention. When his fingertip glided over a taut nipple, she arched her back, pushing her breast into his palm.

"I wanted you in that elevator. Backed against the wall and wrapped around me." The confession left his mouth before he could censor it. Sheiks did *not* make confessions that left them vulnerable.

Maybe she didn't hear him.

"I thought you were too hot to be real," she admitted. "I was running from Husam."

He stilled, blood thrumming in his temples. "He pursued you?" Rage filled him cell by cell. "Why didn't you tell me until now?"

"He didn't really do anything. What was I supposed to say—that he looked at me funny? I did tell you that."

"Yes." Tariq held her tightly. "If anyone else looks at you in a way that makes you feel uncomfortable, I want you to tell me that, too." Unreasonable jealousy gripped him. He knew he was scowling, but couldn't help it. He held her tighter.

She smiled.

"I'm serious."

"I know. You look pretty fierce."

"Husam wanted you for himself, and called ahead to make sure you were saved for him." Tariq's jaw muscles tightened even more.

She shuddered, probably thinking the same thing he was—about what Husam would have done with her, and what would have happened to her once he had grown bored with his new toy.

"You're determined to fight?"

"It's inevitable. If we don't push the bandits out, our tribal lands will be overtaken before we know it, our people killed, and our impressionable young recruited."

Sara wrapped her arms around Tariq and pulled him to her, no doubt to distract him from thinking about the coming battle. He let her. He was more than willing to forget for a single night, a night spent in her arms.

He kissed her.

"I want you," she whispered, then smiled against his lips.

Tariq wanted to make her happy, to keep her happy. For as long as he could. The way his life was, he couldn't promise forever. But for as long as fate would give her to him...

Her hand sneaking under the waistband of his pants cut off all further thought. She wrapped her slim fingers around him in a surprisingly firm grip that made him worry about how long he was going to last. "Easy, love," he whispered.

She let go at once and was pulling away, but he stilled her. "I just meant I want to savor this for as long as we can."

She smiled again.

He slipped off his robe and tunic, then shed his pants, never drawing so far back that he lost contact with her hands. No way was he giving that up. Then they were naked, pressed together, her leg thrown across his, his mouth fused with hers, their bodies tangled in pleasure.

He turned her on her back and dipped to taste her breasts as he positioned himself between her legs. She opened for him, sending a new surge of desire to his core.

But when someone cleared his throat just outside the tent flap, they jumped apart.

"Sheik Abdullah, forgive the intrusion." The voice was Nawfal's, tight with tension.

Tariq sat up and pulled his shirt on over his head, following dark premonitions. "What is it?" He dragged up his pants, casting one last look at Sara before heading outside. He wished to return soon, so they could continue where they had left off. But Nawfal's tone of voice had left him little reason to hope.

"The sentries?" he asked the man, wanting whichever guard had seen something to be brought to him for questioning. He could see nothing in the moonless night save the nearest tents and Nawfal, who was now shaking his head, keeping his gaze on his feet.

Tariq's blood cooled rapidly. "All of them?"

"Yes, Sheik."

Dead. The night guards were already dead. Tariq swore fiercely under his breath. "How many enemies?" he asked, wanting to know what they were facing.

"At least forty," Nawfal said gravely.

"What are they waiting for?"

"I don't know, Sheik."

"And our men?"

"Waking up and arming as quietly as they can. I sent word to the other tents as I came to yours."

"You stay with her," he said, and nodded in approval when Nawfal sat cross-legged in front of the tent, his AK-47 laid across his lap.

Tariq sneaked off into the darkness and rounded the small camp, keeping in the even-darker shadows of the tents. He counted five trucks. How was that possible? They must have rolled in with their engines turned off. He couldn't see any men save those in the cabs, but was sure the backs were filled with bandits.

Maybe they were waiting for reinforcements, maybe for word from their leader. In any case, his people didn't have much time left. He crept back the way he'd come, relieved Nawfal, telling him to be ready, then slipped back inside the tent.

Sara was dressed and ready for action. He handed her one of the handguns, kissed her fiercely on the mouth, then blew out the light.

"The bandits are here. We are surrounded."

And Karim wasn't here with the reinforcements yet. Allah help them, they weren't ready.

Chapter Ten

She'd been told to stay in the tent, but she couldn't do it. If death was coming for her—and seeing the bandits' handiwork before, helping to bury the victims, had left her with few illusions—she at least wanted to stare it in the face instead of huddling in some corner.

Even if the bandits meant to take her instead of killing her, she made up her mind not to go. She didn't care for the fate that would await her there. She would live with Tariq or die with Tariq.

She ran among the chaos of a camp preparing for attack, women and children scampering, men dashing from tent to tent, distributing weapons. Tariq's figure wasn't hard to find. A good head taller than the others, he stood as unmovable as the boulders of the oasis, the sole point of stillness in the melee.

Military trucks and pickups, along with a couple of Jeeps, surrounded the camp in a near perfect circle, each vehicle filled with armed men. She couldn't quite make out how many. It was still early and there wasn't enough light.

"I need another gun," she said once she reached Tariq.

"Go back to the tent." His eyes swam with regret, the set of his mouth fierce as he pulled her behind the water truck he'd been standing next to. There weren't a great many things in camp that could be utilized as effective cover. Some Bedu were using their camels.

"Is the tent bulletproof?" She glared at him. "I'm not going to be any safer there."

"We need only to hold out for a few hours. Karim and our corporate security force will be here," he said, then added, "I'm sorry."

"It's not your fault."

"I should have been able to protect you."

"Why?"

He stayed silent for a while, then murmured, "Because I'm the sheik." There was a world of misery in his voice.

"Exactly. You're not king of the universe, or savior of all."

He didn't respond, just shot her a dark look.

"I want to be able to defend myself." She didn't say, *I want to be able to defend you.* Sara fully intended to watch his back, but knew enough not to push him too far.

And it worked, because he shouted to a young man running by them. The youth slid an AK-47 off his shoulder—he was carrying a half-dozen—and handed it to Tariq, who passed the weapon to her.

"I'm sorry," he said again.

"Be sorry quietly," she snapped. "Because I really don't want to hear it."

He smiled at her then. Probably at the bizarre picture she presented in her exquisite Bedu robe, with the beat-up rifle at the ready.

"You truly are a lioness," he said.

"Yeah. Hear me roar and all that." Despite the tense situation, the vibes of the coming violence in the air, she smiled at him.

His chest expanded as he drew a slow breath. He opened his mouth to reply, but was cut off by someone shouting from the top of one of the vehicles that surrounded them.

She recognized two words, Tariq's name and hers.

"What does he want?" she whispered.

Tariq waited a beat. "Wants to talk to me." He wouldn't look at her.

"I know you've been living here for a while, so let me refresh your memory about American women. Nothing pisses us off as quickly as some macho man lying to us to protect us." Sara was proud of the steel in her voice.

There was silence in the camp, and enough

tension that she wouldn't have been surprised to see the air crackle with lightning.

Tariq passed her his handgun, then his own AK-47. "I'm going to talk to him."

"No."

"There are women and children in camp," he said simply.

Meaning they had to try to avoid an open fight at any cost, delay an armed confrontation until their backup got here.

"What did he say about me?"

"It doesn't matter. You're nonnegotiable."

And he wasn't?

"No." She tried to block his way.

"Do you trust me?" He held her gaze.

Oh, great. He had to put it like that. "I trust you with my life," she said carefully. "I'm just not sure if I trust you with yours. You're liable to try and do something heroic."

He smiled, then turned quickly and left her.

She peeked under the water truck and followed his progress as he made his way to one of the enemy trucks. He held his hands out to show that he was unarmed. Every weapon the bandits had was aimed at him.

When he reached them, two men jumped to the sand. They turned him and slammed the butts of their rifles into his back, searched him for guns before forcing him to kneel in the sand, facing the camp.

"Sara Reeves, you foreign whore, come out," someone shouted in English now.

"No!" Tariq roared, the first word he'd said to his captors. He tried to struggle to his feet.

But more men ran to hold him down, two shoving their rifle barrels against his temples, one on each side.

Nawfal shouted something in Arabic—an order to attack?—but the whole camp seemed frozen in shock.

Then the bandits opened fire on the tents. Only in warning, it seemed, as they stopped after a few rounds. Terrified screams erupted. Women and children came rushing out in confusion, then rushed back in when they realized they would be even easier targets in the open.

Sara dropped her weapons and stepped away from the water truck.

"No," Tariq shouted, his face twisting with desperation and anger. "Don't do this."

Only half of the bandits' guns were trained on him now. The other half pointed at her.

She was grateful that the dress she wore hid her shaking steps, her trembling limbs. She knew what would happen when the bandits had them both. Still, the loss of two lives seemed better than the loss of several large families of Bedu. She understood why Tariq had handed himself over. She couldn't do less.

She'd never been so frightened in her life. It seemed that ever since she'd entered the desert she'd been in mortal danger. She would have probably died ten times over by now if it hadn't been for Tariq.

She walked up to him and dropped to her knees on the sand.

The look in his eyes promised the apocalypse.

And it started right there and then.

He threw himself backward, grabbing a rifle barrel in each hand, drawing the men who held them with him. The weapons were his before anyone realized what had happened, the men dead. He somehow managed to grab Sara, too, and they rolled under the nearest truck with lightning speed.

The bandits were shooting, but slowed as one screamed over the din of weapons. No doubt yelling at his men for aiming at his truck, killing his own men with misdirected bullets. Fortunately, nobody came to look for Sara and Tariq under the truck.

The Bedu warriors of the camp opened fire, drawing the bandits' attention. The air was filled with battle cries and death screams, the smell of blood and gunpowder thick in the air.

Sara huddled behind one wheel, blindly squeez-

ing the trigger of the rifle Tariq had given her.
Several moments passed before she realized she
was wasting bullets. She paused then and took more
careful aim, imitating Tariq, taking shallow breaths
to avoid the exhaust that poured from the tailpipe
of the idling truck.

If a bullet didn't kill them, the exhaust gases
might, given enough time. She turned her face toward
the slight breeze that brought fresh air from the front.

The Bedu kept the bandits so busy they stayed
flattened in the truck bed, not keen on jumping to
the sand and looking around. But now and then
one sent a line of bullets through the sheet metal
platform, hoping to hit Sara and Tariq. They were
hiding in the worst possible place: under a truck
that was full of their enemies.

None of the bullets came anywhere near, but
Sara cringed and flattened herself to the ground
each time, until Tariq pointed upward.

"We are next to the gas tank. They're not going
to shoot at it."

Not unless they were ready to blow it up. Under
different circumstances, she might have relaxed a
little. But in her current situation, with one way to
die crossed off a list of a hundred, it didn't seem
like much of an improvement. But at least she
stopped anxiously waiting for the next attempt
from above, and focused on aiming and shooting.

God, the air beneath the truck stank. Then they got a reprieve as most of the bandits' trucks began to move forward, except for the few pickups that had been eliminated by the Bedu. Since the old Russian Kamaz military truck they were hiding under had pretty high road clearance, they were able to walk in a crouch under the slow-moving vehicle and briefly keep up with it, staying in cover of the giant tires. The bandits must have been linked by some sort of communication system, either radios or cell phones. This sure looked like a coordinated attack.

The air quality improved even more as the truck advanced. Sara and Tariq both crawled forward, trying to keep up. She had no doubt that men up top were watching and waiting, planning to shoot the second the two of them were exposed.

The chance finally came to duck out and roll behind the cover of some goat pens they were nearing. A hail of bullets followed them, but none found their target.

The bandits crisscrossed the camp, knocking down tents with their vehicles, riding over the wounded with glee. But the Bedu fought with twice the passion. They fought for justice and for their families, while the bandits fought on their leader's order. Little by little, the tide seemed to turn.

Sara picked off a bandit who was aiming at one

of the tents, then smiled in triumph when she realized the Bedu were winning.

Though the trucks had advanced in an orderly fashion, they withdrew in confusion. She was backing away from one coming her way when the steel of a gun pressed to the back of her head stopped her abruptly. She glanced at Tariq, to find that he was being jumped, as well. When the man who held her life in his hands shouted in Arabic, Tariq raised his hands and dropped his weapon, then folded to the sand when several rifle butts slammed into his head and back.

Sara's own gun was twisted from her hands, and she was grabbed and tossed into the bed of a moving truck, despite her desperate struggle to break free. She had barely pulled herself to sitting when Tariq was dumped next to her. The two men who vaulted up behind them wasted no time. One held a gun to Sara's head while the other bound their hands and feet.

Tariq spoke rapidly in Arabic, probably trying to bargain or threaten. The men's only response was to kick him as the truck picked up speed, leaving the din of the battle behind. Whoever wanted them must pay enough to make his men intent on delivery.

At first the bandits watched them closely. But after a while they grew bored and settled down behind the cab to talk.

"How are we going to get away from them?" Sara whispered to Tariq, who was lying next to her, leaning against the tailgate.

"We wait. If one of them comes close enough, I'll attack. You pull yourself up and climb over the tailgate."

"You'll follow?"

He nodded. "When I can. Keep going if you get free. Don't wait for me. I'll find you."

Of that, she had no doubt. He seemed fiercely determined.

But the men paid little attention to them, not even when, after a while, Tariq began goading them. They played cards and, when she figured the time was nearing noon, they drank and ate, offering nothing to their prisoners. Then they played cards again. Eventually, one of them settled down for a nap. The other kept his gun close and a sharp eye fixed on Sara and Tariq.

Now was the time. Now or never.

"Pretend you're sleeping, too," she whispered to Tariq.

He searched her gaze, not looking happy with the idea, but after a few moments did as she had asked.

Sara rolled to face the bandit, letting her robe fall open at the front. The man's eyes widened, and he leaned forward. She stretched, as if trying to get some relief for her back, allowing her breasts to press against the light fabric of the dress she wore under her robe.

After a moment of hesitation and a glance at his buddy, the man stood.

She smiled at him.

He smiled back and came closer.

She smiled wider when he leaned forward and reached with his left hand to fondle her breast, keeping his gun aimed at her with the right. She pushed forward as if enjoying it.

Quick movement came from behind her as Tariq seized the man's extended arm and pulled him forward, butting him with his head. The bandit lost his balance and folded over without a sound.

"We have to go now." Tariq shoved him off Sara. "I didn't appreciate what you were doing, by the way." He scowled, but was going for the metal pin that held up the tailgate. She went for the other. They were lucky that their hands were tied in front of them and not behind their backs. When they had loosened the pins, they lowered the back carefully, making sure they didn't wake the sleeping guard.

They had a gun now, but a gunshot would alert the men who rode up front in the cab. A silent escape was by far preferable.

Tariq took the gun and shoved it into his belt. "We'll jump on three."

Then she noticed the large bloodstain on his sleeve. "Your wound opened."

He shrugged.

"What's wrong with your leg?" She caught sight of more blood just above his knee.

"Stray bullet," he said, as if it were no big deal.

She hadn't realized he'd gotten hit again. She wanted to shake him, and she would. If they stayed alive. "You could have told me," she muttered.

He flashed her a look that said *What could we do about it?*

And she hated that he was right. The sooner they escaped, the sooner he could get help somewhere. "One, two, three," she whispered.

He jumped. She hesitated. The truck was going fast, the ground far away, the sand studded with rocks. Tariq rolled, then came to a halt, looked after her with urgency in his gaze.

A good fifty feet separated them by now.

Jump, jump, jump. She took a deep breath and went for it, but was yanked back hard enough for the air to leave her lungs. She was suspended in midair, facing the rapidly moving ground. A moment passed before she realized that she hadn't been caught by one of the men, but by her own dress, snagged on the tailgate. She wiggled, but couldn't tear free.

Tariq was two hundred yards away now. He

had struggled to his feet and was coming after her, but with his legs tied together he wasn't making much progress.

She swung her body and managed only to rattle the tailgate, so stopped immediately for fear of waking the bandit. If she stayed quiet, at least Tariq could escape.

The distance between them was growing rapidly. Her clothes, which held her weight, tightened around her stomach, and the movement of the truck made her nauseous. Soon, Tariq disappeared from sight. Fear gripped her.

She wanted to scream with frustration, feeling dizzy from the blood rushing to her head. By the time the truck stopped, several hours later, she was on the verge of passing out.

The sleeping guard woke and shouted immediately, rushed to grab her. He unhooked her clothes and let her drop to the hard ground. He was next to her soon enough, yelling at her and kicking her. She curled up in a ball, grateful that her limbs had gone numb and could feel little pain.

Others came with guns trained on her.

"Please don't shoot," she begged, with all the hopelessness she felt.

THE ONLY THING that kept him alive was the hope that she had somehow broken free. The fact that they hadn't met yet only meant that she had some-how wandered off the trail left by the bandits' tire tracks. Tariq pushed forward.

He would find her. He scanned the sand for foot-prints. The air was still and stifling, but he didn't mind. He prayed for the continued absence of wind—a wind that would obscure the tracks he followed.

He could have walked back to camp. That probably would have been smarter, since it was closer. Except that he could not make himself walk in the opposite direction, away from her. The drop to the ground had opened his wounds further, and they were bleeding freely. He felt weak and dizzy, dehydrated. He ignored all that and marched on. The desert might kill him yet, but not today. He was going to find Sara.

The tire tracks seemed to converge in front of him. He blinked his eyes until they went back to normal. He put one foot painfully in front of the other. If he was a good Muslim, he should be able to accept Allah's will. But he could not submit to death, not yet.

He'd been a fool and he didn't want to die a fool.

He'd come to Beharrain out of duty, but had never acknowledged, not even to himself, that he loved his people and loved his country. He'd wanted to win them over by producing results. He'd wanted to impress them with his Western knowledge. And all this time, all they had wanted was to know that he cared, that he had their best interests at heart, that he would lead them with integrity and protect them from attack, like the sheiks of old.

He loved this land. He would gladly give just about anything for it and his people. But not Sara. He would never give her up, not even out of duty.

Tariq kept her face firmly in his mind as he stumbled forward. He didn't hear the trucks until they were upon him. He had no weapon, no strength to fight. The only thing he could do was march stubbornly forward.

But as the vehicles slowed behind him—he didn't look back; he was nearly beyond rational thought, moving on sheer will—the hail of bullets didn't come. Then he was surrounded by familiar faces, faces etched with concern.

"You will be well. We'll take you back." Someone was already bandaging his arm with a kaffiyeh.

"No." It should have been a sharp command, but the single word came out a whisper. He gripped the nearest hand as hard as he could. "Sara," he said, and did his best to convey his emotions with his eyes.

"Doctor first," Karim said.

"Sara." Tariq would not drop his gaze, more scared than he'd ever been that his brother and his men would not go after her.

Chapter Eleven

"So this is the foreign whore who bewitched my son?" The shah spoke English, even though he was addressing the guard. Probably so she could understand and be further intimidated.

He could have spared the effort. She was frightened out of her mind already, waiting for her fate in the dark of the cave. There had been choppers in the air, presumably looking for her, so her captors decided to wait until dark before moving on. They even pulled their vehicles into the giant cave situated low on the hillside.

"My son wanted to make you his mistress. You did not deserve the honor." The man spat at her.

There were other men sitting in a semicircle around her. They were laughing.

"Please. I didn't do anything." She had a fair idea that they meant to kill her, but could think of no way to save herself. She had to delay, stay alive until they made a mistake, and the smallest chance for getting away presented itself.

The older man the others called "Shah" kicked her, bruising her knees.

"You mesmerized my son. Bedeviled him. It is because of you Husam is dead," the shah shouted. He nodded toward the guard again.

The man grabbed her from behind and pulled her toward the cave entrance. Below the hill the terrain flattened out fast, an oil well reaching to the sky less than half a mile from them. She couldn't see much beyond that in the settling dusk. One of the men backed a Jeep out of the cave. The shah got in next to the driver. Another man grabbed her and shoved her into the rear, climbing in after her. She looked around for any sign of rescue as they rode toward the pump, but could find none. The well area seemed deserted, save for a handful of bandits.

She didn't have to wonder long what their plans were. The men tied her to the pump, then someone brought a rucksack, put plastic explosives around the base and began hooking up the wires.

"Please don't. This will only hurt your own people." She was frantic with fear now and not above begging.

They went on as if they hadn't heard a word she said.

When they were done, the shah stepped up to her

one more time. "I would hope to send you after Husam to serve him in paradise, were you a virgin. But as I very much doubt that, know that I'm sending you to hell."

HE HAD RESTED ALL DAY in the back of the chopper as they looked for her, his wounds treated. By the time they finally spotted the truck near an out-of-the-way oil well, Tariq felt much stronger. Not that lack of strength could have stopped him. He would have crawled across the sand if he had to.

"Do you see her?" he asked Karim, who was piloting the helicopter.

His brother shook his head, then called over the radio to the other two choppers. One was the corporate helicopter, the other sent unexpectedly by the Tihrin police. The gesture seemed odd due to the fact that the police had no real authority outside of the city, and certainly not in this part of the desert. The authorization for their mission had to have come from far above, perhaps as high as the king.

It could be that the monarch didn't want news of an American businesswoman's kidnapping to mess up the international relations he'd been so tirelessly building. Or he may have been influenced by his American-born queen. Tariq wasn't about to worry about motives. To save Sara, he would gladly take any help he could get.

"Farther back," he said, when Karim began to descend, appearing ready to set the chopper down in the middle of the gathering of bandits, who were shooting at them already.

His brother corrected the direction, with a scowl on his face. He had murder in his eyes and a Magnum stuck in his belt. He had taken Aziz's death even harder than Tariq. The two had been twins, and together all their lives, while Tariq had just recently gotten to know them both.

"Whoever killed Aziz will die by my hand," Karim declared as he lowered the chopper to the sand.

Tariq grabbed his guns. "Don't expect me to start asking questions. Whoever gets in my way, I'm shooting." Then he was out of the chopper before the rotor blades had a chance to stop spinning.

He ran toward the well, not bothering to look for cover; there was no place he could have hidden on the flat sand, anyway. Tariq hoped the gathering darkness and the fact that he was constantly in motion would be enough to foil the bullets that flew in his direction.

Karim caught up within seconds, a sign of how much blood Tariq had lost, how weak he really was. He ignored the thought.

Whoosh. A shoulder-launched grenade sliced

the air between them, the force of the explosion knocking him face first to the sand.

They no longer had the chopper.

Tariq came up to his knee, then pushed himself to standing, sparing but a glance at the wreckage and Karim. "Okay?"

His brother swore darkly and set off at a run, with single-minded determination.

Tariq moved the other way, keeping low, aware that they were both outlined by the flames behind them, and had just become easier targets. He kept firing, forcing the bandits to take cover behind the trucks, careful not to hit anyone who might be hidden inside. He still hadn't seen Sara. He did see men fall, however, and he kept track with grim satisfaction.

"Sara!" he called out, but no answer came. He didn't allow himself to think that he was too late.

He finally reached a small, corrugated-aluminum utility hut, and ducked behind it. Over the barrage directed at him, he could hear gunfire from the other side of the well, no doubt involving Karim. Where were the other two choppers? The helicopters had split up the desert terrain for the sake of efficiency, the obvious drawback being that they couldn't provide each other with backup now.

Where was Sara?

Tariq ducked around the side of the hut to scan the area. And when he finally spotted her, his heart stopped, because he spotted the wires at the same time.

Who had the button? What was he waiting for?

His question was answered shortly when a voice called out in Arabic from the darkness.

"My son is dead because of her. By law, her life belongs to me," Omar said.

He was speaking of the old Bedu law—a life for a life.

Omar. The man who had been a father to Tariq in place of his real father over the past four years. The betrayal cut him to the quick. And he knew in that instant that Omar had been behind the attack on the convoy, behind the explosion at the other well. He was building an empire by tearing down Tariq's.

"My brother is also dead. Let this stop here," he replied, although, despite his Western upbringing, he was too much Bedu to let it go so easily. The rage he felt over Aziz's death only intensified.

Omar must have suspected as much, because he didn't bother to answer.

"I will pay the blood price." Tariq tried again. If a man was killed, his family might forgo revenge if restitution was paid to them.

"You will pay with your own blood," taunted Omar. "You and your last brother. You shouldn't have come here."

Did Omar want to be sheik? Tariq considered that possibility for the first time. Where on earth would he come up with that fantasy? He was no blood relation. He had been captain of the guard at his father's palace before rising to his current level of success at MMPOIL.

Where was the man? Tariq peered in the direction of the voice, but couldn't see him. All he needed was one lucky shot. Omar's hodgepodge of followers wouldn't be brave enough to go up against a sheik without their leader. But Tariq could see no sign of the man.

And he couldn't leave his cover and come out into the open. It was a miracle he hadn't been hit making his way over here.

He judged the distance to Sara. Could he reach her? But again, he would be out in the open and provide Omar with the convenience of being able to kill them both with just the push of a button. Tariq clenched his jaw. Allah, but he wanted to be by her side!

Now that he was out of reach, the bandits stopped shooting at him, but they were still firing at Karim. How was he holding up? Tariq wished they could communicate.

If his brother shot into the fuel tank of the truck Omar was hiding behind, the explosion would either take care of the man or stun him long enough for Tariq to get to Sara. But there was no way to tell Karim to do so.

They needed another plan, one that would work with the few meager tools at Tariq's disposal. That gave him a thought. He shot at the men to distract them for a second, then, under the clamor of return fire, busted the lock off the utility shed door with his rifle.

Not much was in there but some basic tools and—he felt a quick burst of hope—a three-gallon can of gasoline. Tariq ripped a strip of cloth from his shirt and tucked it in, making an oversize Molotov cocktail. Then he lit the end of the rag and ran.

The shed blew sky-high, like a rocket.

He used that distraction to make his way to Sara. She was barely visible, the brightly burning shed casting her in deep shadow.

He had her ropes sliced and the cloth out of her mouth in seconds, brushed his lips against hers briefly as he grabbed her by the arm to take her out of there.

"You'd better not." Omar stood not ten feet from them. He must have run forward to check on her.

"If you ignite the charge, you will die with us," Tariq said, pointing out his mistake.

But Omar didn't even flinch. There was nothing but hate in his face. "You shouldn't have come back to this country, Brother," he told Tariq. "And you…" He spat toward Sara, but was too far away to hit her. "You should never have come here."

"'Brother'?" Tariq laughed.

"The first son," Omar said, with contempt in his eyes. "I'm the first son of our father. The first son from a maid, long before politics forced his four wives on him. A son never acknowledged, but no less important. He was a nineteen-year-old prince when I was born and a fifty-year-old king when you came along."

"You lie."

Omar growled in anger. "Our grandfather would not let him acknowledge me. Then he couldn't later, when he became king, and the moral compass of the country. But he took care of me."

"That's how you became captain of the guard at the palace." Tariq still didn't quite believe him, but was beginning to understand.

"Guarding your mother, who was the favorite wife, in place of my own." Omar spat again. "I thought our father's successor would come from there. I did my best to stop it. Do you remember your other brothers?"

Barely. They'd died young from accidents and childhood diseases. Except that now Tariq was beginning to wonder.

"You're crazy," he said, stunned that the man could have hidden his scheming for so long, could have accomplished so much destruction.

"Crazy like a fox." Omar grinned, seeming satisfied with himself.

Tariq thought of the accident that had cost Aziz his leg and Karim his eye, and he was certain now this man had been behind those, as well, and behind all the sabotage that plagued his businesses. Omar wanted to discredit Tariq before the tribe.

"You went against your own people."

"They'll be better off with me. I've waited long enough. I would have convinced our father to acknowledge me and appoint me to the throne, had Majid not gotten in the way. He was even more bloodthirsty than I was. Should have paid more attention to him when he was a child."

The buzz of a chopper came from the west, clearly audible over the shouting of the bandits, who had just noticed their leader's precarious position.

No shots were forthcoming now. Omar stood between the targets and his men.

Tariq glanced toward where he'd last heard Karim. Had his brother witnessed Omar's confession? Or had he been hit? Tariq's chest squeezed tight with anger at this man who was putting all he held dear in danger.

"It's over," he told Omar, training his gun on the man and holding Sara tightly to him. He could feel her heart beating wildly against his side.

Gunfire started again, but not aimed at them.

Omar's men were shooting at the descending chopper, the Tihrin police. The policemen weren't shy about returning fire, and unlike the corporate choppers, their helicopter sported a convenient machine gun protruding from the nose.

The first round of bullets hit a gas tank and blew up one of the trucks. Bandits were running away from their vehicles now, racing toward their leader. Tariq only hoped the reinforcements realized they were at the well, and wouldn't blanket the area with fire.

"Don't shoot. We are here," he called to them, with little hope of being heard over the din.

Another truck went up in flames, outlining Karim's limping form. That had been his work.

All weapons were quiet for a moment, the opposing forces at an impasse. Some of the bandits were looking sideways more than at their leader, giving the impression that they'd just as soon slink away into the night, at the first opportunity.

"Back off! Everybody back up or I'll blow the well," Omar shouted, and held up the small black box in his hands.

"Drop it." Karim's voice was as hard as the alloyed steel of the pump, his tone as dark as crude oil as he appeared close behind Omar, seemingly out of nowhere.

The man seemed stunned, clearly not having

expected this turn of events. He had a hard time accepting that control was fast getting away from him.

The sound of trucks broke the momentary silence.

Allah help them if more bandits were on the way! Tariq thought. He stared at Omar, who didn't look any more hopeful than a moment before, his face still tight with hatred and desperation.

Who else could be coming?

Both sides waited, wondering the same. The air fairly crackled with tension as guns were raised, ready to fire. Tariq pushed Sara behind him. But when the first shouts reached him, he recognized the voices of several men from his tribe.

Apparently Omar, too, understood that this was now the end for him, because he pushed the button.

One full second passed before the explosion. Enough time for Tariq to fly across the sand with Sara—it was hard to say who was dragging whom—and flatten them both to the ground.

Oil and sand flew toward the sky, then showered back down around them. Then fire, fire was everywhere. Even the sand seemed to be burning, as were their clothes. Tariq rolled onto Sara to smother the flames, before allowing her to help him.

Karim was there then, extending a hand.

"Come, Brother." And then they were running for the police chopper.

But a quick escape from the inferno was not to be had. The bandits who were still alive were fighting his men now, wanting to seize any trucks that were whole, since theirs were on fire. Several bandits were running for the police chopper, too.

Tariq picked up a gun from the sand.

"What now?" Sara asked, coughing from the smoke.

Tariq's tribesmen were arranging themselves around her, Karim and himself.

"Now we fight," he said.

He kept one eye on her and one on the enemy as they cut a swath through their opponents. The heat was unbearable. Time lost all meaning.

At first, the bandits had the upper hand, but slowly the tide turned. And after another bloody half hour, Tariq thought they might even stand a chance. Then he saw Omar—his robe charred and still smoking, the left side of his face bloody—going for the police chopper, and he ran for the man. Out of the corner of his eye, he caught a glimpse of Karim doing the same.

"Mine!" Tariq's brother issued a fierce battle cry. He gripped an old-fashioned sword in one hand—he must have gotten it from one of the fallen of their tribe—and his gun in the other.

For a moment, Tariq was willing to fight him for the privilege, the Bedu blood rising in him. But then he heard Sara calling his name from behind, and turned to help her, leaving Omar to Karim.

SARA COULD DO NOTHING but stare as Tariq walked toward her, leaving the chopper that sat on the sand a few hundred feet away. She was resting by the water's edge at the oasis, still shaken from the battle that had ended no more than an hour ago.

Tariq's traditional Bedu clothes were a little worse for wear, seen in the light of the full moon above them. And she couldn't help but smile. The sheik and his chopper, instead of the sheik on his Arabian horse—her girlhood fantasies updated for the twenty-first century.

Except that this was no longer a fantasy, and the reality was grander than anything she could have imagined. Tariq was a better man than she had ever met in life or in the pages of a novel. He was strong, good-hearted, honorable, complex and passionate. She swallowed at that last adjective, fighting to put some heated memories out of her mind.

"How did you learn to pilot a helicopter?" she asked as he dropped to the sand beside her.

They had been on their way to Tihrin when he'd asked if she would mind if he set the chopper down for a few minutes. She didn't. She knew too well that once they reached the city their paths would diverge. She wasn't ready to say goodbye to him yet. Although she wasn't sure whether these extra stolen minutes might not make parting all that much harder.

"Karim learned first. And then Aziz. And then they talked me into it." A sad smile hovered on Tariq's lips as he remembered Aziz. "That's how badly we couldn't trust anyone. We had to make sure we could protect ourselves."

"I can't imagine living like that." She thought of Karim's role in saving her, and felt grateful to Tariq's brother. He was scary, that one, and the scars on his face weren't the least of it.

"For the most part, I didn't have to. My life in America was pretty ordinary."

She seriously doubted that, but didn't say anything.

"Thanks to my mother," he added, and shook his head. "All this time, deep down, I had been mad at her for sending me away. When I was young I thought that meant she didn't love me as much as she loved my brothers and sisters." And then he proceeded to tell her what he had learned from Omar.

Her eyes teared up from the tale, as Sara felt his pain and that of the courageous woman she had never met.

"You know, at one point the uncle who raised me hinted at possible danger, but I didn't want to believe him. I was a teenager filled with anger. I thought that if there truly was danger, then she was making a coward out of me by keeping me away because of her own fears. If I had to die for my country, I was ready to do so."

"And now?"

His masculine lips stretched into a rueful grin. "I'm beginning to see the value of being alive. I learned things while living abroad that can aid my people. I can help make the transition easier as they learn to function in a world that works with different rules than they are used to. Hopefully, I can make them see that they have many other treasures beyond the oil, a lot to offer the world."

Hearing him say the words with conviction left no doubt in her mind that he was an exceptional sheik and exactly what his people needed.

And she needed him just as much, a little voice in her head insisted. She did the best she could to drown it out, almost succeeding until he drew her into his arms, terminating all her valiant efforts.

His dark eyes searched her face. "I don't want you to leave."

Her heart rolled over in her chest at his quiet intensity.

"Leave here?" Did he want them to spend the night at the oasis? Because she wanted that, too, one more night in his arms.

"Leave *me*." He dropped a gentle kiss on her lips.

Could he mean what she thought he meant?

She didn't have a chance to ask before he kissed her again.

This one started slow, but gathered heat quickly as he proceeded to claim her mouth. Her muscles had gone soft with need by the time he pulled away.

"It is not finished between us," he said with determination.

"No." No sense denying the obvious. She snuggled into his warmth.

"You'll stay?"

She nodded against his chest, and he tightened his arms around her, letting out a deep breath she hadn't realized he'd been holding.

"How is this going to work?" she asked.

"You wanted to take your company global. You can open your new international office in Tihrin and run it."

That could work, but it wasn't what she had meant. "Between us."

He lifted her chin so she would look into his eyes. "The Bedu in me wants to kidnap you and claim you as my wife and never let you go."

The breath caught in her throat at the untamed edge in his voice.

"The Western-raised side reasons that it's too soon, that it wouldn't be what a woman of your culture wants, that we should take it slow. Will you agree to give me time so I can prove to you that we belong together?"

"Yes." She didn't think she was going to need all that much persuading.

He traced her jaw with his thumb. "You humble me with your trust and loyalty." He kissed her again.

Amazing that he could still think, because she had passed that point five minutes ago. She could do nothing but feel—his firm lips on hers, his tongue teasing her own, his hands sliding up and down her arms as he caressed her.

Heat built inside.

"I want you," she admitted hesitantly, when the ache within her reached an unbearable level. From what she'd read, Arabic men preferred shy women and were repelled by brazenness, but she couldn't help herself. She was who she was. If he was serious about a relationship between them, he would have to learn to live with it. "I want you," she said again, and splayed her fingers across his wide chest.

"Allah be blessed," he said, with such relief it made her laugh.

He helped her out of her clothes, then she helped him out of his. His body looked magnificent in the twilight, strong and stalwart, corded with muscles. She gently glided her fingers over his scars, some of which he had suffered for her. His wounds had been sewn up. They didn't mar the wild beauty of his warrior's body; they gave him character and a dangerous edge.

He dipped his head to kiss a distended nipple, and she moaned, first in pleasure, then in protest, when he broke the kiss to lift her and carry her into the pool. The sound of the gurgling stream was music for them, the warm breeze caressed their skin, as did the water, which was a comfortable temperature from the day's heat.

And his hands on her…

Sara's senses were stimulated on every front. Her senses and her heart.

"Do you believe in love at first sight?" he asked as he nibbled her neck.

"Not outside of my favorite books." Love took work and sufficient time for the parties to get to know each other.

He moved up and swirled his tongue around her earlobe. "I'm going to make you believe in it."

She was too weak with pleasure to fight him. He was not the type of man to be deterred from his goals in any case.

Did she love him? Was she falling? He was an honorable man who had earned her respect and ad-miration. Okay, so maybe love, too. Maybe they were heading that way. She grew thrilled at the thought. One thing she knew—there was no one she would trust more with her heart.

She wrapped her legs around his waist, and he pressed forward. The hard feel of him against her opening brought a wave of exquisite pleasure. And when he pushed inside, stretching her, filling her, she had to hold on to his shoulders for support.

The water carried some of their weight, making them feel light as they glided against each other with tantalizing ease. He claimed her lips and greedily swallowed her little moans.

He held her up with one hand and explored her body with the other, while she caressed every available inch of him, hardly daring to believe that they were here, together like this. That he was hers for the night and possibly for many more nights to come.

But soon she had to let go of her delicious expectations of the future, because the present was demanding all her attention, her body tightening with pleasure, forcing her to focus on the moment and nothing beyond. And what moments they were!

Tariq must have been losing some of his measured control, as well, because his easy movements picked up more speed, more force. They clung to each other, feeling as if they couldn't get close enough. He ground into her deeply, and Sara groaned, arching her back and neck, lifting her face to the starry sky. It seemed impossible that her body could feel this much pleasure and not burst with it.

If he weren't holding her up, she would have drowned. Her muscles were well beyond control. But he held her and kissed her, touched her just where she craved to be touched. When heat burst inside her, and her body contracted around him, she felt his immediate response. The intensity just about blinded her, and must have deafened her, as well, because when she could finally function again, he was looking at her expectantly. He must have asked a question without her hearing.

"*Will* you stay the night with me here?" he asked. "For a night, with myself and nobody else?"

"Yes." She understood what he wanted. She wasn't ready to return to the real world just yet, to her hotel, not even if he was coming with her. The silence of the desert around them was spellbinding, fostering the feeling that they were the only two people in the world.

He carried her out of the water and laid her gently on the sand. "Will you stay with me in Tihrin?"

He hadn't said *in my palace,* but she knew what he meant, thought it endearing that he was still un-comfortable with all the splendor being a sheik entailed.

"Yes."

He kissed her then, and after a while, made love to her again. And again.

Epilogue

Tariq wanted to take her on a round-the-world honeymoon, but Sara insisted on going to the Oasis Resort. The luxury complex had been nearly completed in the past year while Sara flew back and forth between the U.S. and Beharrain, setting up an office near her new home in his palace. She left the original office in the care of an excellent manager. MMPOIL was her biggest client at the moment, hopefully soon to be followed by more Beharrainian petrol companies. He was proud of his wife.

They had fallen behind schedule on the last two buildings because at the last minute, when an old-fashioned well had been dug between the two for the tourists' amusement, an underground cave system had been discovered in the rock base under the sand. The caverns and passageways were even now being mapped and considered as an addition to the novelties the Oasis would offer.

The landscaping was in place, the green grass and the palm trees nodding in the wind, the Middle Eastern architecture of the villas and the main hotel breathtaking, as were the natural-rock swimming pools that glistened in the sun.

"Ya noori." He'd never said those words to any woman but her. *You are my light.*

She knew their meaning and smiled, rolled toward him on the luxurious divan that took up one whole corner of the room in the villa where they had once hidden from the sandstorm.

Tariq was happier than he'd ever dared hope to be. He'd found someone in life who could be his true partner, a woman he could love, trust and cherish until the end of his days. "I love you more than words can say in any language."

"I love you, too." She smiled.

He cupped her face and kissed her, got lost in her desert honey sweetness. They lay in each other's arms, replete from their lovemaking. He wouldn't have minded staying like that for hours yet, but breakfast today was going to be served by the pool, and had promised to be a grand affair. The French chef the king had loaned them for their honeymoon would have had his feelings hurt if they didn't show.

"We should dress before we get distracted. Again." Sara pulled away, her tone teasing but her smile very satisfied.

He planned on keeping her smiling like that for decades to come. He helped her pull a long, richly embroidered dress over her head, unable to resist caressing her curves through the soft material.

She slapped his hand playfully, but laughed out loud. "You'd better eat and regain your strength first," she said as he stepped into his own clothes.

"Nothing wrong with my strength." He pulled her close to prove it.

Excited shouts from outside drew their attention. What was it now? Tariq stepped to the door, then took off running toward one of the buildings under construction, where he saw workers gathering, some gesturing wildly.

"Stay here," he called back to Sara. Had there been an accident? Was someone hurt?

"What happened?" Of course Sara, as always, was right behind him.

They were about a hundred feet from the small crowd when an explosion shook the air. Like missiles, bricks came falling from the sky. He ducked, pulling Sara with him, protecting her as best he could. He would have thought that with Omar gone there would be no more sabotage. More than ever, he wanted peace.

Odd about the bricks, he thought then, confused. The building that had blown up was constructed of steel-reinforced cement. Where had the bricks come from?

He reached for the one at his feet, knowing what it was even before he wiped it on his pants. A gold bouillon bar. The shower of debris stopped, and he moved toward the hole in the ground, watching for anyone who needed his help. But although the people were covered with sand, they all looked unharmed—and as stunned as he was.

Sara reached for his hand and he walked with her, knowing it would be useless to talk her into seeking safety. She stood by him, no matter the circumstance.

People were running toward them to make sure he and his new wife were well. He assured them they were, and pressed on, stopping only when he could see the crater the explosion had left behind. Thousands of gold bars lined the hole, some melted, others unharmed, glinting in the sun. Their hiding place had obviously been booby-trapped.

"What on earth is this?" Sara asked, wide-eyed.

A few men were already climbing down, calling out with excitement at the discovery.

"Majid's gold," Tariq said, and grinned, pulling Sara close to him.

"The rumors were true," she said, dazed. "It wasn't just a myth. What are you going to do with it?"

"It belongs to the whole country. The gold will solve a lot of people's problems, and for that I am happy." He brushed his lips over hers as he tight-ened his hold on her. "But as for myself, I already hold my treasure in my arms."

* * * * *

*Don't miss Dana Marton's next
Harlequin Intrigue book in April 2008,
when 72 HOURS,
a romantic thriller, will be on sale!*

REQUEST YOUR FREE BOOKS!

2 FREE NOVELS PLUS 2 FREE GIFTS!

HARLEQUIN®
INTRIGUE®

Breathtaking Romantic Suspense

YES! Please send me 2 FREE Harlequin Intrigue® novels and my 2 FREE gifts. After receiving them, if I don't wish to receive any more books, I can return the shipping statement marked "cancel." If I don't cancel, I will receive 6 brand-new novels every month and be billed just $4.24 per book in the U.S., or $4.99 per book in Canada, plus 25¢ shipping and handling per book and applicable taxes, if any*. That's a savings of close to 15% off the cover price! I understand that accepting the 2 free books and gifts places me under no obligation to buy anything. I can always return a shipment and cancel at any time. Even if I never buy another book from Harlequin, the two free books and gifts are mine to keep forever.

182 HDN EEZ7   382 HDN EEZK

Name	(PLEASE PRINT)	
Address		Apt. #
City	State/Prov.	Zip/Postal Code

Signature (if under 18, a parent or guardian must sign)

Mail to the **Harlequin Reader Service®**:
IN U.S.A.: P.O. Box 1867, Buffalo, NY 14240-1867
IN CANADA: P.O. Box 609, Fort Erie, Ontario L2A 5X3

Not valid to current Harlequin Intrigue subscribers.

Want to try two free books from another line?
Call 1-800-873-8635 or visit www.morefreebooks.com.

* Terms and prices subject to change without notice. NY residents add applicable sales tax. Canadian residents will be charged applicable provincial taxes and GST. This offer is limited to one order per household. All orders subject to approval. Credit or debit balances in a customer's account(s) may be offset by any other outstanding balance owed by or to the customer. Please allow 4 to 6 weeks for delivery.

Your Privacy: Harlequin is committed to protecting your privacy. Our Privacy Policy is available online at www.eHarlequin.com or upon request from the Reader Service. From time to time we make our lists of customers available to reputable firms who may have a product or service of interest to you. If you would prefer we not share your name and address, please check here. ☐

HI07

the DEVIL'S footprints

Don't miss the latest thriller from

AMANDA STEVENS

On sale March 2008!

AMANDA STEVENS

the DEVIL'S footprints

MARKED BY EVIL

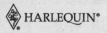

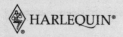 **HARLEQUIN®**

INTRIGUE®

COMING NEXT MONTH

#1041 POINT BLANK PROTECTOR by Joanna Wayne
Four Brothers of Colts Run Cross
When Kali Cooper inherits the Silver Spurs Ranch, she isn't prepared to find a murdered woman there, or the wealthy rancher next door. But Zach Collingsworth can be counted on when all the chips are down—and it looks like it's Kali's time to cash in.

#1042 GUARDIAN ANGEL by Debra Webb
Colby Agency
No one knows who the Guardian Angel is or where he comes from. But to rescue six missing children, investigator Ann Martin will have to break her own rules and trust a vigilante who operates on the other side of the law.

#1043 UNDER HIS SKIN by Rita Herron
Nighthawk Island
Nurse Grace Gardener brings Parker Kilpatrick back from the brink of death, only to seek his protection. On a collision course with two killers who want their secrets kept, Grace recruits the one detective with the brass to stop them.

#1044 NEWBORN CONSPIRACY by Delores Fossen
Five-Alarm Babies
Mia Crandall and Logan McGrath are about to have a baby. Except they have never met. Now they must work together to save their child, but can they survive the frightening conspiracy behind their unplanned union?

#1045 SET UP WITH THE AGENT by Lori L. Harris
With her cover blown, China Benedict is targeted for death. But she survives. Now FBI counterterrorism expert Killian James will put his life on the line to keep China out of harm's way in order to recover a stolen biological weapon.

#1046 FORBIDDEN TOUCH by Paula Graves
Away from the prying eyes of the world, Iris Browning and Maddox Heller are both looking to bury their secrets. Instead they find each other. Yet the closer they get, the more dangerous their attraction becomes—until it isn't something either can easily walk away from.

www.eHarlequin.com

HICNM0108